LOST AND FOUND

by

Vivian Roberts

Dales Large Print Books
Long Preston, North Yorkshire,
BD23 4ND, England.

British Library Cataloguing in Publication Data.

Roberts, Vivian
    Lost and found.

    A catalogue record of this book is
    available from the British Library

    ISBN   978-1-84262-741-9 pbk

First published in Great Britain in 2008 by Black Star Crime

Copyright © Working Partners 2008

Cover illustration by arrangement with Arcangel Images

The moral right of the author has been asserted

Published in Large Print 2010 by arrangement with
Harlequin Enterprises II B.V./S.à.r.l.,

Dales Large Print is an imprint of Library Magna Books Ltd.

Printed and bound in Great Britain by
T.J. (International) Ltd., Cornwall, PL28 8RW

LOST AND FOUND

With special thanks to Jean Davidson

To my writing buddies–
thanks for your incredible support.

PROLOGUE

Life could turn on such tiny events as matters of timing. If she had been five minutes earlier, or five minutes later, that Tuesday morning, Natalia would never have been drawn into the search for a missing person.

'Baker Street, this is Baker Street, change for the Metropolitan and Jubilee Lines...'

While the morning rush-hour crowds surged out of the Bakerloo Line train, hurrying through archways, down tunnels and up stairs, Natalia took in the scene, even managing to catch her early-morning glimpse of Sherlock Holmes; his distinctive profile with deerstalker hat and meerschaum pipe outlined on decorative tiles along the platform. How she loved the old Baker Street station, which belonged to another era, with its dark-brown wood fascias, old advertising hoardings, and grand entrance hallways lined with shops and cafés. But there was no time to dawdle. London was an impatient and demanding child, as was Avon, her boss at the Lost Property Office, who would have a fit if she was late.

She bent to give a coin to Homeless Joe, who was in his usual pitch by the station entrance. And perhaps she would have walked right on past the man with his canvas bag filled with rolled-up posters, if it weren't for one thing: his Oxford brogues.

Slowing down, her clear gaze took in a smartly dressed man in a business suit with an attaché case between his tailored trouser legs. His shoes spoke of money and under-stated style, his suit of Bond Street. Hardly the garb of your typical illegal fly-poster. But what drew her attention most was a quiet desperation in his manner, and the speed with which he worked.

Lord, could this be the Hoaxer himself? Ever since she'd come to work at the Lost Property Office a few months back, she'd heard of little else. So far the Hoaxer had baffled her superiors with his increasingly daring practical jokes revolving around lost property and posters with ransom demands, but was the mystery about to come to an end? They'd all believed it was an inside job, but was the Hoaxer getting more audacious, and recruiting?

From the corner of her eye, as she drew nearer, Natalia glimpsed the distinctive blue-and-white jacket of a Transport for London official moving in on the man.

The man, who looked to be in his thirties, turned and Natalia saw that he was un-shaven, his thick, dark-brown hair unkempt, at odds with his business clothes. This was not the face of a practical joker, but the drawn features of a man in anguish.

'You'll have to take these down, sir. What you're doing is illegal.'

Natalia was dimly aware of the official reprimanding the man, as her attention was swallowed up by the image on the poster. It was of a woman in her late thirties, about the same age as herself, with light-brown, high-lighted hair, wearing distinctive hooped earrings and a highly decorative silk scarf in ochres and oranges wound round her neck. It could have been bought in a North African bazaar, or just as easily in Camden High Street. But more arresting than that was the wistful look Natalia recognised in the woman's sad, hazel eyes; a sense of longing with which she was only too familiar.

'Please, I have to put these up. Can't you look the other way for once?'

'I'm sorry, sir. Unauthorised postering is not allowed.'

'Let me explain. It's my wife – she's missing.'

As the man rubbed a hand over his stubble, Natalia noticed his smooth hands were well manicured, the hands of an office worker. Hunched over, he looked so despondent that Natalia's heart went out to him.

Ignoring his pleas, the Transport for London official simply reached up to tear the poster from the wall. As the other man moved aside, Natalia got a clear view of the words underneath the picture: 'Missing for five days – my beloved wife, Helen Bookman. Have you seen her? If you can help, please phone her husband, Peter.' Followed by landline and mobile phone numbers.

Natalia shivered, although it was not a cold day. In a city the size of London, Helen could be anywhere. Anonymous. Alone. Unseen, despite the millions around her.

'You can tear that down, but I've got plenty more. You won't stop me!' The man – Peter Bookman – called after the official, who shrugged and said, 'Move along now, please,' and walked away.

As she watched, Peter's defiance left him and his shoulders slumped wearily. Natalia caught his eye and connected with an emotion she thought she understood only too well. Losing someone was the worst kind of pain. Smiling kindly, she went up to him.

'Can you give me a spare poster?' she asked. 'I work at the Lost Property Office near here. I can put one up. It might help.'

Some of the frustration left his gaze. 'Thank you,' he said. 'Here, have several. I've had to print them up myself.'

'You've contacted the police of course.'

'Right away. But the police just aren't interested – they told me to wait, see if she came home.' His voice was hoarse but she detected a refined London accent. Close up she saw his pale-blue eyes were bloodshot. 'I've spent hours on the phone – friends, family, hospitals. Nothing. The police don't care. I just want to know my darling Helen is safe–' His voice cracked as he put out a hand to touch her photograph. 'I can't bear to be doing nothing.'

Natalia took two of the rolled-up posters, the paper shiny beneath her fingers. 'I will tell all my colleagues–' But just then two British Transport police strolled up.

'Come along, sir, move on. You're blocking the entrance.' They stood either side of Peter, determined to make him leave. He looked diminished between them. Defeated, he allowed himself to be escorted away, but not before he gave Natalia a last, grateful glance.

Natalia sighed deeply. Reconnecting people to lost objects – objects to lost people. This was something she could do, something she was good at. If she could be of any help to the Bookmans, any help at all, she would do it.

1

Stepping through from the vault and main office into the Lost Property Office's grey-carpeted reception – a pair of Jimmy Choo shoes in hand – Natalia knew that she'd made a spectacular error. One look at Avon's face told her that.

The vault was where all lost goods were stored after cataloguing. It was ruled over by Cliff, a grim-faced Scotsman whom she'd only exchanged brief, businesslike words with. On those rare occasions, he'd had a tendency to raise his voice at her. Natalia quickly came to understand it was nothing personal. It was his custom to raise his voice with any foreigner who came into Lost and Found, as if by shouting the words they would be better understood. She didn't blame him. This custom was common whether you were in Poland or Turkey or England, or anywhere in the world. Give him time, she thought, give him time.

Unusually, however, Cliff had not been patrolling his domain, and neither was his Serbian assistant, Stefan, anywhere to be seen. At risk of incurring Cliff's uncertain temper, she had made her way through his domain without permission.

But it was the fury in Avon's brown eyes that halted Natalia in her tracks now. Was it really so awful that she'd broken protocol? she thought. It had been impressed on her when she'd first joined that each employee at the Lost Property Office had their assigned role and to cross boundaries was frowned upon, but surely when she explained the unusual circumstances Avon would relent?

16

'What have you been doing?' Avon demanded, her podgy hands planted on her wide hips. Even her magenta hair seemed to flame with disapproval. Natalia recognised the signs: Avon was stressing again. Judging by the expressions on her colleagues' faces, they'd already been made aware of it.

She hesitated. It seemed everyone was in reception, all nine members of staff, instead of one person manning the desk where members of the public showed up in search of their lost property. Cliff, the keeper of the vault, who had been nowhere to be seen when she'd ventured in search of the shoes, had returned. Perhaps he'd been on a ciggy break outside. He was listening in openly, his small eyes hard, she noticed with a sinking feeling. Mark Thomas, the cheeky young Londoner who kept her amused with his banter, was waggling his finger at her, behind Avon's back, silently mouthing the words 'tutt, tutt'. He was almost schoolboyish, with his light, curly hair and slightly chubby figure – but his youthful charm had more to do with his attitude than his appearance. He was forever teasing Natalia and mocking Avon behind her back, and he had his impression of their boss's 'you're in big trouble' act down pat. Natalia had quickly grown familiar with this expression on starting her job. Mark often joked it should be Avon's screen-saver.

17

Natalia looked around for her friend Stefan. A young Serb, they'd become fast friends and not just because they were both from Slavic-speaking countries. He was in reception, too, but his lean, toned figure was standing to one side, studying some papers from a file in his hand. He was tall and handsome, with the sort of rugged dark looks that revealed his Eastern European origins. His chiselled features were focused on the document in his hand, but when she glanced at him she saw him look up, meeting her gaze with his dark-blue eyes.

And then a shrill voice with a cut-glass accent piped up from behind them all, declaring, 'This kind young lady has been looking after me.'

Natalia watched as everyone turned to face a woman standing at the public counter.

'Natalia is not authorised to–' Avon began, flushing pink with annoyance, but stopped abruptly when the woman, in a most unorthodox fashion, proceeded to lift one bare foot onto the counter.

'Someone stole my shoes–' But upon spotting the make of shoes in Natalia's hand, she hurriedly lowered her foot and swooped on them. In a trice they were on her feet. Natalia noted with pleasure they matched the older woman's suit, too. She'd been so relieved to find a pair of nice shoes in the size the woman had told her. She'd chosen well, and they had just reached the end of their three-month hold date today, so were due to be auctioned off anyway, if unclaimed.

'Perfect.' The woman beamed. 'I'll make my appointment now. Thank you ever so. I think this is going to be my lucky day.' She stood up, slapped a ten-pound note on the reception desk, surprised Natalia by shaking her hand, and then was through the automatic doors, walking as if she'd owned the shoes forever.

'Another victim of London Underground's Shoe Fetishist,' Natalia explained. 'No one was around when she came in. I couldn't send her away with bare feet.'

'It's clever stuff, stealing shoes on tube trains in broad daylight – or should that be broad electric light.' Mark laughed, amused at his own joke.

Natalia smiled, but no one else did.

'If folk are careless enough not to hold on to their shoes, more fool them,' Cliff grumbled. 'People will get away with anything if you let them.'

'It's no laughing matter.' Avon fixed Mark with her angry, beady-eyed gaze. 'You, Cliff, should have been in duty in the vault. As for you, Natalia,' she pulled herself up to her full five feet one inch and looked up at her, 'you've overstepped the mark.'

Natalia braced herself for more, trying not to smart at Avon's words. She glanced towards Stefan for support, but he had gone back to what he was reading, seemingly engrossed. The silence that followed was worse than the telling off she expected. Avon now ignored her, busying herself instead at the computer terminal on the reception desk, muttering under her breath, 'All this extra work, and now I'll have to do a report as well.'

A report, Natalia shook her head, for sending a customer away happy? Or a report about Natalia breaking the rules! She had a sudden sinking feeling. So that was why the others were still hanging about. They were waiting to see what Avon would do next.

'You've done it now,' Mark said, chuckling. He was standing next to her, his voice low so Avon couldn't hear. 'I'd say you were up to your neck in it.'

'Up to my neck in what?' Natalia whispered back. She still couldn't understand what the big deal was.

'You mean you don't know the secret of yon shoes. The ones you just gave away?' Cliff joined in, so all could hear. Natalia glanced nervously at Avon's back, hunched over the computer, but the other woman just ignored them. 'Me and the lad here,' Cliff nodded Stefan's way, 'had special instructions to look after those shoes for a certain lady boss of yours. Isn't that right, Stefan? They were spoken for if unclaimed.'

'Oh, I had no idea.' Natalia groaned inwardly. Now she'd be on Avon's bad side permanently.

'Ignorance is no defence. Not when you've come between Avon and those shoes. That's right, isn't it, Avon, those were the Jimmy Choos you've been lusting after? The ones you hoped wouldn't be claimed?' Cliff brushed aside Natalia's explanation, his attention fully focused on Avon's back.

Avon did not deign to reply. Tossing her head, she finished up at the computer, then put the ten-pound note away in the cash box. Natalia knew that was a fair fee for the shoes, as they normally charged one pound for umbrellas or books, and up to twenty pounds for electronic equipment such as laptops.

'Stop lounging about in reception and get back to your desks,' Avon finally retaliated, whirling around. 'The public will be intimidated if they see you lot when they come in.'

Natalia automatically glanced towards the big, automated glass doors, which opened from reception directly onto Baker Street. Her view of the street was obscured either side of the doors by old-fashioned display boards. These exhibited to passers-by in the street all manner of lost items both historical and modern. Dull, grey carpeting, which Mark referred to as 'standard airport' surrounded the simple desk, where members of the public applied for objects they'd lost on train, bus or taxi. It was neither grand nor imposing, but a friendly welcoming space for even the most shy of customers.

Avon disappeared through the gap in the office dividers behind the reception desk, into the open-plan office beyond.

'Don't be a sore loser, Avon,' Cliff said, following her and running his hand over his short, bristly, grey hair. 'The lassie didn't know you'd set your heart on those heels. I'll find you another pair, what d'you say?'

'Oh, get back to work, Cliff. They were only a pair of shoes.' Avon refused to look at him.

Cliff stopped, his face returning to his more usual dour expression. 'OK, I can see you've so many, far more important, things to attend to,' he muttered. 'We all know you're too grand for the likes of us...'

Avon must have heard him because she turned beetroot red, changed direction and hurried towards Donna, who was just emerging from the vault. Donna Harris was her direct superior and headed their entire department. There was some truth in what Cliff said, Natalia thought. Avon did spend more time seeking Donna's approval than getting to know her staff.

Was Avon angered or embarrassed by his remark? They all knew she was easily wound up, Natalia thought, but why would Cliff want to wind her up even more? Cliff, though, did not look pleased at the reaction he'd got. His expression more grim than ever, he strode across the office towards the entrance to his 'kingdom', the vault, saying, 'Don't hang about, laddie,' to Stefan.

Natalia exchanged a wry smile with Stefan, who had now put away the papers he'd been reading and tucked the file under his arm. They threaded their way slowly through the desks. 'Is he always like that?' she asked. 'It's the first time he's ever addressed me directly. Well, he wasn't really speaking to me. He was getting at Avon. But why?'

'He loves his job. It is his wife! He is very good at it, no surprise. He does it for twenty years or something.'

'Twenty years – he must love it. What did he mean about Avon's important work? Finding our office hoaxer?'

'No, no,' he laughed. 'He says to me she spend all her time tracking the designer labels that come in. She comes in the vault to look at clothes, jewellery, and her favourite, shoes. We joke, maybe she is Shoe Fetishist. Cliff has, as the English say, a real chip about it. To him, only doing your hard work is what counts.'

'I wonder how he puts up with you then, little brother number one. Always checking your appearance in the mirror,' she teased.

'I must keep the girls happy, cheeky! What you think of my new jeans?'

Natalia looked her friend up and down. He was tall and lean, his narrow hips fitting snugly into his tight jeans. He wore a striped blue shirt, as always outside his jeans and open at the neck, showing just the right amount of dark chest hair. But it was his eyes that made women turn their heads. A dark, navy-blue fringed with thick, dark lashes. His black hair was cut short and he usually styled it with gel. He definitely knew how to dress.

'As good as the last pair,' she reassured him.

'Ah, those were my lucky jeans,' he sighed. 'They had many stories to tell.'

'What Mark would call your pulling pants.' Natalia grinned. 'I think I'm glad all that is behind me now.'

'While I am still enjoying having adventures. Well, must go, or Cliff will be in worse mood and find me horrible jobs to do.'

He made his way past Mark's desk, which was nearest to hers. Beyond lay the desks of Poppy, Jim and Ranjiv, whom she had yet to get to know. She saw Stefan place the folder he'd been studying in reception on the corner of the desk as he passed, without comment and without Mark looking up. He paused in the wide entrance to give her a quick wave, then disappeared behind the floor-to-ceiling metal grille, which obscured the shelving beyond.

Natalia headed back to her desk past Mark's, making a detour to avoid bumping into Avon and Donna who, deep in conversation, were now moving towards Donna's glass-partitioned, corner office. To her surprise, Mark hurriedly covered up the papers he'd been writing on, and then pushed them into a folder. It was the same one Stefan had placed there a moment ago.

'All right, Nat?' he said.

'Natalia,' she corrected him mildly. When he looked up at her like that, all innocence, he reminded her so much of her younger brother when he'd been particularly naughty. Ginger, with freckles, and cheeks Natalia's mother would forever have been squeezing, he had a cheeky, wide-eyed gaze which made him look twelve years old rather than his actual twenty-five.

'Don't worry about that report. Avon'll get a bee in her bonnet about something else in no time.'

'Bee in bonnet?'

'Get in a flap, in a tizzy, knickers in a twist.'

'Twisted knickers!' Natalia was glad he'd paused. She still found it hard sometimes to follow his rapid-fire, East end of London accent. Though he'd told her he wasn't a true Cockney. 'Not born to the sound of Bow Bells, I'm just a regular short-arsed geezer,' he'd said incomprehensibly.

'Donna's desperate for us to win "Best Lost Property Office of the Year" and knock Manchester off their perch,' he went on, making a face. 'Seriously, we've more chance of beating Man United at Wembley. But inside that well-honed body of hers beats a heart of pure ambition!'

'You think they are talking about that now?' They looked over to where the two women stood by the door to Donna's office. The big rings on Avon's hand flashed as she gesticulated, still pink in the face, looking up at her boss. Natalia thought that this week's magenta-coloured hair suited her better than last week's McDonald red. But then, that wasn't saying very much.

Donna, as always, was meticulously tailored, not a sleek blonde hair out of place, though there was something different about her today – yes, she was wearing her hair loose, and a mid-length black skirt instead of trousers. Natalia wondered what might have warranted this change, but Donna's expression gave nothing away. Natalia found the difference between the two women intriguing: Avon rarely sat still for long, she rustled and paced and zoomed about like a busy bee. She became easily stressed and emotional. Donna, on the other hand, was cool and collected, her mind always on the bigger picture. Donna was a woman who pushed herself too hard, and Natalia sensed her mind was fixed on the goal, never the journey. In her thirties she looked younger than Avon, who was ten years her junior. Natalia had caught the incorrigible Stefan admiring her trim and athletically-fit figure.

'That, or our resident hoaxer. He's got them pretty annoyed,' Mark reverted to the office's usual topic of conversation.

'You think the Hoaxer's a man?'

'Got to be – it's a bloke's sense of humour, ain't it?' He winked, leaving Natalia uncertain whether he really meant what he was saying. The British sense of irony was still sometimes too alien for her to grasp.

'Whoever it is has a weird sense of humour.'

'You saying us blokes are weird?'

'Of course!'

'I'll tell you what's weird. Whoever is nicking them women's shoes? Did you hear London's *Time Out* magazine has dubbed him the "Shoe Fetishist". The guy must have the sleight of hand of a magician. What does he do with them? The mind boggles.'

'Drink champagne out of them?' Natalia joked.

Mark smiled back at her. 'Ugh, imagine the taste. No, someone with a Cinderella complex!'

'Someone who wants to open their own shoe shop.'

'Or make a sexy film about stilettos.'

27

'OK, the thief only takes high heels so ... it's a transvestite who's too shy to go into a ladies shoe department.'

'OK, I can't beat that, you win the point this time.' Mark held his hands up in defeat, grinning.

Laughing, Natalia moved on, as the two women carried on talking. Neither had looked in her direction and she hoped Mark was right and this morning's incident would blow over. However, they had been looking very conspiratorial. Natalia enjoyed her new job, the people she worked with and prided herself on her work. It was never easy moving to a new country, and even harder to connect with new people. She was making some good friends here and didn't want to jeopardise that. For her, people would always come first.

Taking one of the posters of Helen Bookman from her desk, she looked around the office. Where would be the best place to put it so that everyone would see it? The office noticeboard was on one of the dividers, just by the exit to reception. Everyone had to pass that way, so it would be the ideal place. As Donna entered her office and Avon made her way back to her desk, which was close by, Natalia pushed home the drawing pin and smoothed down the paper, looking again into Helen's sad eyes. Missing five days, so she'd disappeared last Friday.

From her husband Peter's demeanour it was clear she'd acted out of character. But before Natalia could think about it further, a shriek caused her to whirl around and see everyone's heads in the office snap up

What the hell?

Natalia exchanged a startled glance with Mark and the others in the office before they were all on their feet and heading for Donna's office, intrigued at the prospect of a second break to their routine.

2

Natalia peered over Ranjiv's shoulder as everyone crowded in the doorway. It was the first time she'd seen the inside of Donna's office close up. There were the standard office grey goods – filing cabinet, freestanding cupboard – as well as more personal touches: an ultra-modem coat stand with her coat hung neatly on a hanger, photographs on the walls, and a brilliant-orange bird-of-paradise plant, which stood in a big, white china pot beside Donna's desk. A reminder of Donna's South African roots.

'What's happening?' she heard Stefan's voice behind her ask. So, was it Avon's or Donna's scream that had reached him in the vault? Both women looked outraged, and both were holding what Natalia immediately recognised as the handiwork of the Hoaxer.

'What's he said this time?' Mark said in her ear.

'She, it could be a she,' Natalia returned. 'Women can make jokes, too.'

'Is it you then?' He dug into her ribs with his elbow. 'Confession time?'

'Come in, everybody,' Donna beckoned before Natalia could think of a retort. 'I want you all to see this latest piece of nonsense.' Her accent was more pronounced than usual, Natalia noticed, betraying agitation beneath her cool exterior.

As they all squeezed in, Natalia found herself standing next to Donna, beside her desk. There was just room for them all.

'What's this, a Mother's Union meeting?' The sardonic comment came from the doorway, which was filled by Cliff's solid frame.

'It's no laughing matter, Cliff,' Donna said sharply. 'Show them, Avon,' she went on. 'We each found a hoax on our desks. This was mine.'

She held up the Hoaxer's trademark: a sheet of paper bearing an enlarged photograph. It was of a pair of Impala horns. Scrawled in felt-tip pen across the bottom were the words 'You give me the horn!' and two kisses.

Avon then held up hers. It depicted an

impressive leather diary. Scribbled over it was the line 'I'm late, I'm late, for a very important date!'

Avon was notoriously punctual. She'd once set three alarms, programmed the telephone, and asked a friend to phone her – only to find she'd turned up a whole day early for her training exam.

Now either the Hoaxer didn't know her at all, or was getting a dig in, which seemed the more likely explanation.

Natalia felt, as much as heard, Mark's quickly stifled guffaw of laughter. She was aware, too, of Stefan's darkly comic grin.

'That's a big pair of horns,' he called out, and now it wasn't only Mark shaking with laughter.

'It's an outrage!' Avon could not contain herself any longer. 'Someone in this office is taking personal swipes at us. And you all know I'm never late.'

'Aye, you're always rushing about too fast to be late,' Cliff said, all seriousness, but Mark shook with even more laughter and Natalia saw Stefan's grin widen.

'Thanks, Cliff, but that doesn't help at all,' Avon spat back. 'I want to know; exactly what you are doing to stop this idiot?' She tossed her photograph down on top of Donna's on the desk and glared at Cliff. 'The Hoaxer is stealing items from your precious vault, from right under your nose. You can see the LPO tags on them.'

'Woah,' Cliff held up his hands. 'I'm a stickler for the rules and I don't care who knows it. But Stefan and I canna be everywhere at once in that vault. It's too big. You canna accuse us of not pulling our weight, like some I could mention.'

'We're not into the blame game today,' Donna said to defuse the tension, leaning forward to pick up the photo Avon had just discarded. As she did so a waft of warm perfume, exotic and musky, reached Natalia's nostrils. She's got a hot date tonight, she thought.

'How many hoaxes does this make now?' Donna asked.

'Five,' Mark replied.

'Six,' Natalia corrected quietly.

'Well, it's five or six too many now,' Donna began but, before she could go on, an argument broke out over the number of hoaxes so far.

'Avon had the one with the spectacles–' Mark said, ticking hoaxes off on his finger as he listed.

'Saying "I've got my eye on you". It's true. She's always saying that.' Natalia stepped in.

'And Donna had the one about–' Jim began.

'Cliff had one, too,' Stefan reminded them.

Cliff shrugged his shoulders. 'A pair of bagpipes "Blow one for me" or some such

32

nonsense. I tore it up.'

'You should have kept it,' Avon rounded on him. 'We need the evidence.'

A sudden loud bang silenced the voices.

'This is not helping, as Avon rightly pointed out earlier,' Donna said, putting down the stapler she'd rapped on her desk.

'Somebody is making a mockery of our work, and thinks they can run rings around us,' Avon said. 'It's one of us. These messages are *meant* to be personal.'

Everyone started studying the carpet thoughtfully, glancing slyly at one another through corners of eyes.

'You all know what I have to do next,' Donna said. 'I've got to call the police in again. I have to report thefts from our vault, and as none of the items has been returned yet, it technically is theft.' She sighed. 'And as my secretary, Rose, is away on holiday, I'll have to place all those calls myself.'

'Don't worry, Donna, I'm going to find out who's responsible,' Avon said, face alight with the desire to please her boss. 'I'm going to stop them in their tracks. If you'll let me, of course. I'll introduce a package of measures, tighten up security. In fact,' Avon rushed on, raising her voice, 'if the Hoaxer dares to steal another piece of lost property, I'll catch them red-handed.'

'Uh, well done, Avon, for that initiative,' Donna said. Natalia, standing so close, thought she caught a flicker of annoyance in Donna's eyes. Maybe she didn't appreciate being forced into supporting her deputy. 'Though I'm sure the police are quite capable of–'

'And when I do, they'll be getting the sack. On the spot!' Avon was quite carried away now. Had she gone too far?

All eyes switched to Donna now. Two spots of colour showed on her cheekbones. 'That would be for our superiors upstairs to decide, Avon,' she said sharply, then hurried on as Avon's face crumpled. 'But you are right to mention the possibility. Now back to work, everyone. Playtime is over for today. I've got a phone call to make.'

As they all trooped out, Natalia noticed that while Mark went ahead, cracking jokes, Stefan couldn't resist glancing at his reflection in the glass door to check his appearance. Natalia paused with him.

'I didn't know Cliff had received a hoax. I thought only Donna and Avon got them.'

Stefan grinned and winked. 'Maybe he sent it to himself. Like a Valentine. He didn't want to be left out.'

'Horns, what a hoot! Impala, they're from South Africa aren't they? The Hoaxer knows his stuff. Sorry, his or *her* stuff,' Mark said, backtracking to them and nodding at Natalia, as the rest of the staff started wandering back to their desks. 'I had a hoax, too, right at the beginning. Football scarf. Arsenal it was. I ask you, and everyone knows I'm a Tottenham man,' he said scornfully.

Natalia led Mark and Stefan over to the noticeboard, ignoring the repartee that broke out between the two young men about who would come out on top if Tottenham and Crvena Zvezda were to play a match. 'OK, little brothers one and two. I want to show you something. See this poster? I pinned it up just now. I want everyone to be aware of it, so tell your friends. The contact numbers are on the bottom here.' When she turned to face the poster, she was struck anew by the forlorn look in the missing woman's eyes. 'Her husband is desperate to find her. He has not seen or heard from her since last Friday.'

'What do the police think?' asked Stefan, his voice soft now.

'He says they say he must wait for her to turn up.'

'Perhaps she's had an accident,' Mark speculated, all joking aside for once.

'He will have phoned all the hospitals,' Natalia said, thinking he'd probably be phoning them every day, just in case.

'She could be leaving her husband,' Stefan suggested thoughtfully. 'What is he like?'

Natalia thought of the distraught, unshaven man she'd seen a few hours ago.

'He's lost his world.'

Sober now, the two young men returned to their work, and she to her own desk.

Throughout the rest of that afternoon, she found her gaze returning to the poster, pleased to see that others in the office were also examining it, wondering over and over, *Where are you, Helen? What happened to you?*

3

Natalia's opportunity to explore and hunt for answers to Helen Bookman's disappearance came much sooner than expected late that afternoon – and she found it in the unlikely and somewhat scary form of Cliff, or 'Mr McDougall to you' as Mark had dubbed him at one time.

After the discovery of the hoax, Natalia found the rest of the workday flew past. She enjoyed the detailed work of assessing each lost item and entering its details on the computer, into the system the Lost Property Office had fondly named 'Sherlock'. And, assuming the mantle of Sherlock Holmes herself, she liked to speculate about the owners. Though, as yet, she had not deduced a one-eyed man with red hair who enjoyed smoking Cuban cigars from anything she'd logged in. If any lost object presented information about the owners – a phone number, e-mail or house address – they had to be flagged up so that Ranjiv's team – Poppy and Jim – could actively contact the owners.

All afternoon, Natalia had been conscious of furious activity on Mark's part. As five thirty approached, she was further distracted by seeing him repeatedly looking at his watch from the corner of her eye. At dead on the half hour, he scribbled some final notes, pushed them into the file Stefan had out on his desk, then leapt up, locked his desk drawers, and rushed out with a careless 'Bye' flung over his shoulder. 'Got a date tonight – Chelsea versus Tottenham .'

That's one key to the English, Natalia thought, their obsession with football, and no one more so than Mark. She knew from her husband that tickets to such matches cost a great deal, especially if bought on the black market. Mark never seemed to be short of money to buy his tickets. But then, although he hadn't told her much about his private life, it had been easy to glean that his idea of a good time was a drink down the boozer with his mates watching football on the pub TV, or attending a live game. Maybe that was why he never mentioned a girlfriend. Would he be prepared to give up some of his football for a girl? She'd have to be very special – or a football fanatic herself.

Natalia glanced at her watch. She still had

a fair few items to get through. She'd been slower than usual today, spending time chatting and going into the vault to help that customer. She'd also been distracted by the hoaxes left for Avon and Donna, but most of all she was bothered by her meeting with Peter Bookman and her concern for his missing wife.

Not one to leave work undone, Natalia decided to carry on and clear her backlog. Dermot wouldn't mind if she was half an hour late home. She'd send him a text, and then he'd have time to chill out with a beer before supper.

The sound of a door closing disturbed her concentration a little while later. Donna's office was still a centre of activity, as it had been all afternoon, with people coming and going. The bottom half of the office walls was panelling, the upper part glass. All she could see were talking heads. Avon and Donna were now closeted with two British Transport police officers; a young female probationer and an authoritative-looking man in his early thirties. It was the same two who had attended after each of the other hoaxes in the past few weeks.

Clearly Avon and Donna had far more important issues to chew over than a pair of Jimmy Choo shoes falling into what Avon deemed the wrong hands. Natalia could relax.

'OK, laddie, don't do anything I wouldn't, now.' Natalia believed she actually heard a chuckle in Cliff's voice. She swivelled in her chair to see him at the entrance to his vault, saying goodbye to Stefan. Cliff glanced disapprovingly round the empty office, barely acknowledging her, then turned back inside. Stefan wove his way to Natalia's desk, a musky scent preceding him.

'You work too hard,' he said.

Natalia made a show of sniffing. 'Mmm, nice aftershave. Smells expensive.'

'I've got to please the girls.' He patted his smoothly shaved chin.

'You play too hard!' she observed. 'Who is she tonight?'

'Oh, I met a nice new girl today, in the bank. Very shapely,' he sketched her curves with his hands. 'Long, blonde hair. We're going to a club, and then – who knows!'

'Don't go breaking too many hearts,' Natalia pretend scolded. Stefan was so darkly good-looking and had such a charming manner that he had all the girls in London swooning for him. Natalia could see in him her own older brother when he was twenty-five. Karl had very fair hair and blue eyes, but was equally charming and handsome.

Karl was the eldest of the four brothers and sisters and their parents had despaired that he would ever settle down – they also feared he'd get a girl pregnant. It seemed there was a new one on his arm every week. He played the field, but never misled anyone, so the girls all remained his friends. Then, one day, he brought Maria to meet his parents and announced she was the girl he was going to marry. And now he was happily married with three young children. Would it be the same with Stefan?

The outgoing Serbian had his serious side, too. He sent money home every month to Belgrade to help his brothers and-sisters through school and university. He'd shown her photos of his dark-haired siblings, all equally good looking, and of the austere block of communist-era flats, where his family lived, crammed into three rooms. 'I made it to university and now London,' he'd said in a quiet moment. 'Best thing for me. I want same for them. Don't tell the others – don't ruin my playboy reputation.'

But Natalia had seen right through that disguise the first time they'd met. They'd clicked as soon as they started talking about their big families back home. Natalia herself had grown up in a block not unlike the one in the photos Stefan had shown her.

Something about her boss now caught Natalia's attention, drawing her away from her reminiscences about Stefan. The policeman and woman were leaving, and Avon stood in the doorway to Donna's office. She was watching Stefan as he swaggered in his jeans and leather jacket out of the office. There was admiration in her lingering gaze. He's definitely not brother material to you, Avon, she thought.

Hearing the arriving rattle of the cleaners outside, Natalia typed furiously for a few more minutes. She had just turned her computer off when a now-familiar, lilting voice said, 'Hi there, Natalia, working late by choice or are you in detention?'

Natalia turned to see a bright-eyed Jamaican woman with a red scarf wrapped around her hair to match her T-shirt and pumps. Her new friend always loved to colour coordinate.

'Rasheda! Hi there, how are you? Time to say hello?' The two women smiled broadly at each other. They both looked over to where the tops of Donna and Avon's heads could be seen still in conference in Donna's office.

'I'm OK for five minutes. Good thing your bosses aren't my bosses. What's going on? I'll have to wait till they're done.' Natalia could listen to Rasheda speak all night, with her rich, buttermilk Caribbean accent.

As senior cleaning operative, Rasheda was trusted to clean the senior executives' offices and had keys to them. Natalia and Rasheda had got talking and laughing together a few weeks before; another time when Natalia had conscientiously been working late. Rasheda

41

was beginning to fill the gap left when Natalia had said goodbye to her closest friend, Marta, when she'd made the move from Warsaw to London six months before.

'Like your top,' Rasheda said, leaning her bottom against Natalia's desk, while her team got to work emptying wastepaper bins, wiping desks and telephones, and vacuuming the carpet. 'That deep-pink suits you.'

'Thank you. I usually get everything at our local market in Hackney, but I went to Monsoon for this. I must find new hairdresser though – my hair is a real problem.' Natalia lifted up her long, pale-brown hair that fell limply to just below her shoulders.

'Not something I can help you with,' Rasheda laughed, signalling to her dreadlocks piled high under the red scarf. 'Tough day? You look knackered.' Rasheda's gaze was concerned.

'Wait till you hear!' Natalia began counting off on her fingers. 'First, I saw this man, Peter Bookman, a husband very upset that his wife is missing There was something special about her–' She did not elaborate. She had not yet confided in her new friend about the events in her past that she was sure drew her to Helen. 'The poster is on the noticeboard.'

'Uh-huh. I'll take a look in a minute.'

'Second, there were two more hoaxes. Some goat horns and a diary! Avon and

42

Donna were very upset. The police were here again.'

'Whatever next, for heaven's sake?'

'And three—'

'Three things! No wonder you're exhausted, chile.'

'I gave away to a customer shoes Avon wanted for herself. She's written a report.'

'Report my ass. That'll go in a file never to be seen again.' Rasheda chuckled.

'But they were Jimmy Choo shoes.'

'Well, why didn't you say? That really is a reportable offence!' Rasheda teased.

'All the same, I hope they're not planning to fire me. I like this job.'

'Honey, they'd be mad to fire you. No one here is as hard-working as you, 'cept maybe that dragon man in the vaults.' The cleaners were not welcome in Cliff's realm, he kept it clean and tidy himself And as Rasheda said before to Natalia, 'Only too pleased not to have to dust all those items – worse than china ornaments!'

'Oh, Lord, here's another visitor. Looks like I'll be working late, too,' she said now.

The stiff, upright figure of a solemn-looking man had entered. He ignored Natalia and Rasheda, knocked on Donna's door, and went in.

'That...' Rasheda said, settling herself more comfortably on the edge of Natalia's desk, and lowering her voice, 'is Omar. How

43

do I know? Well, sometimes I manage to get extra night shifts, and they're over at the CCTV centre, near Bank. I know his wife. She do a few shifts for me some time. Nice woman. Quiet.'

Natalia nodded. She knew Rasheda was always putting in for extra shifts, she needed the money for her younger son's sixth-form-college fund.

'Does Omar work on the CCTV?'

'It's a sad story, it truly is. He's supposed to be a real genius at reading the CCTV screens and working out what's what. He was a top man back in Iran. But then the man who hired him left, and everyone else is too nervous to have a man from the Middle East overseeing all the cameras for Transport for London. Know what I mean? So he's been sidelined into looking at old tapes. Too proud to hand in his notice, though, and they can't fire him.

'Learning to trust, it's difficult, isn't it? If someone wears an army uniform, you know whether he's your enemy or your friend, but otherwise...' she shook her head. 'Get this, he's been told to look over old footage – ha, that's the right word – searching for the Shoe Fetishist! He's head of the Department of Lost Causes, membership one, that's what they say.'

'Please!' Natalia groaned, laughing. 'Why does this shoe thief take just high heels? And

44

they are so bold. They strike any time of the day or night.'

'And where do they keep all their trophies, there must be dozens now. Must be a fetish, what else would you do with hundreds of shoes?'

'And of course they are always glamorous ones.'

'You can imagine how he must hate it. Instead of keeping an eye out for fare dodgers, late-night attacks, that sort of thing, he's looking for someone who gets their jollies from a pair of shoes!'

'He must feel it's a waste of his expertise.'

'The thing is, Omar hasn't discovered any-thing on these tapes. Or so he claims. Now the powers that be trust him even less. An expert like him, surely he'd have gathered some information by now.'

The sound of raised voices drew their attention. Inside Donna's office they could see Omar, Avon and Donna were all stand-ing up, and appeared, to be arguing. Omar was moving his hand in a way that indicated 'no'.

'He's not happy, is he?' Rasheda said.

Natalia thought. 'Perhaps they want him to look for our hoaxer, too?'

'Another insult, he'll think that's child's play. I wish they'd hurry up. I don't want to be late home tonight. My Jason is bringing his new girlfriend Honey home to meet me, so I'd better pretend to be a proper Mum.'

'How's he getting on with his new job?' Jason, Rasheda's older boy, had newly qualified to work in the British Transport unit of the police.

'Loves it! Thinks it's the next best thing to being James Bond. I only wish Daniel had half Jason's dedication. I feel like I'm pushing him all the time, know what I mean? I'm going to have to dip into the fund to get him some private coaching at this rate. He doesn't even try.'

Natalia nodded sympathetically. Daniel was fifteen and a very reluctant school-goer. So far her new friend had not mentioned the boys' father, but it was clear he did not live with them. The whole family depended entirely on Rasheda's cleaning work, though now Jason had started work he would start contributing to the household expenses.

'You'll have to come round, you and Dermot, to my place one night, then we can have a real gossip – oops, I mean talk, of course.'

Just then, the door to Donna's office was flung open with a bang and Omar stalked out, head held high, his expression one of outrage.

'A meeting that didn't go so well. Why do they have all these meetings?' Natalia asked.

'Aye well, it's channels, see.' Cliff's voice from behind them made the two women jump. Natalia had not noticed him come out of the vault. Just how much of their conversation had he eavesdropped on?

'Channels?' Rasheda repeated. She looked curious, and not as surprised as Natalia that Cliff had snuck up behind them.

'You've worked here long enough to know. Departments are not supposed to mingle. You have to go to your boss, who goes to his boss, way up to the top and then the top bosses talk and it comes down the other side. Ruddy nonsense, that's what I think.' Cliff wandered away again, shaking his head, but still lingered in the main office, looking at the poster of Helen Bookman.

Donna and Avon now emerged, wrapped up to go home.

'I think Donna has a date,' Natalia said quietly. 'See, she's wearing a skirt and I smelled exotic perfume on her.'

'Bright-red lipstick, too. Bit of a change from her usual black trouser suits. Wonder who it is? Some high-flier, I expect. She's that ambitious.' They giggled, then Rasheda said, 'I'd better get on now. See you, Natalia,' and she went to collect her cleaning cart.

Natalia put on her coat and picked up her bag, then realised Avon had reappeared through the gap from reception and was calling out to her.

'Yes, Avon?'

'Tomorrow – you report to Omar, the man who just left. He's to open up the old room in the basement here and you're to look at CCTV tapes with him. You're to make sure he finds evidence of our hoaxer.'

'But I don't know how to read CCTV,' Natalia said.

'Omar will give you all the training you need. The technicians have already been in. It's decided.' Without waiting for a reply, she hurried away after Donna.

Natalia took a deep breath. So. She was being transferred. Maybe it would only be temporary. And she'd have a chance to learn a new skill. But how could she succeed where an expert like Omar had failed?

'Ah, hmm,' Cliff was clearing his throat to catch her attention. 'It'll be a change of scenery for you, down in the basement. That room's not been opened up for a while. There's machinery down there, used to be the monitor centre for our CCTV here.'

'I see,' Natalia said, taken aback by his approach.

'If you've got five minutes, why don't you come through and look at the vault. I'll show you around. Give you a better idea of how it all works.'

She was about to refuse, wanting to get home, when she glimpsed something in his face. It reminded her of her mother's uncle. Behind Great Uncle Jan's grumpy exterior lay hidden a vulnerable and lonely old man. Could that be the real reason for Cliff's

48

crusty exterior? If so, and she refused him, he might not allow her to see behind his defences again. There was only one way to find out.

'I'd like that,' she nodded, and followed him into his realm.

4

As they passed behind the metal grille into the vault proper, Cliff's hand shot out in front of her. Natalia halted, all her senses on alert.

'Good old-fashioned bolt,' he said, rattling a very large bolt to and fro in its runners in the grille. 'Can't beat old technology, eh?'

'You lock this every night?' Despite working late on occasion, she had always left before him.

He showed her how the gates closed. 'And unlock it every mornin'. The security guys come round and check it every few hours during the night.'

'Has there ever been a burglar?'

'Burglars! No, but we've had people trying to break in and doss down in the office where it's warm and dry.'

Natalia had a sudden picture of Homeless Joe curled up beside her desk. He'd like that, she thought. She fingered the bolt and padlock, the metal cold and smooth beneath her touch. 'No alarms then.'

'Ach.' Cliff raised his bristly brows. Natalia noticed there was still a touch of sandy colour in the grey. 'I've got one of those. The operatin' box is on my desk.'

'Our office hoaxer must do his work during the day. He'd never get in here at night. You are last to leave?'

Cliff's face darkened at the mention of the Hoaxer. 'Aye. I wait till the cleaners are done and then lock up here, as well as our front entrance onto Baker Street. Yon hoaxer couldn't do his thieving at night.'

Natalia met his gaze. Though his pale-blue eyes were small and hard, she sensed they were a front against the world. Even his clothes hid his real self. A shapeless jumper, usually in some dull-brown or grey, over ill-fitting, baggy, blue uniform trousers. All with more than a trace of cigarette smoke. Why did this man fend off, frighten off even, other people? Did he have something to hide? And why exactly had he invited her on this private tour?

Natalia took a tentative step forward, feeling secure for now because Rasheda and the other cleaners were nearby, and would be for a little while longer. She began to take in the endless rows of olive-green, floor-to-ceiling shelving stretching into the distance, illuminated by overhead fluorescent lightsing.

'Amazing,' she said. 'I'm still officially in training so I have not yet been allowed to take a turn in reception, and come in here to fetch items for the public.'

'Apart from a certain pair of Jimmy Choo shoes,' Cliff observed dryly.

'The shoes, yes.' Natalia couldn't help smiling. 'You were not here. Nobody was in the office. I ran in and ran out.'

'Well, here's your chance to view it properly.' Cliff was not angry with her for coming in unescorted earlier that day and his next words explained why. 'Besides,' he went on, 'it wouldn't have been right to leave one of our customers unaided. But, as ever, initiative goes unappreciated around here.'

Maybe that was his motive. He'd recognised that, even though her clumsy attempt had backfired, Natalia's intentions had been the right ones.

But Cliff was speaking again. 'When I first came here, it was a shambles. I reorganised it all personally. But what thanks did I get? None. Aye, but that's the way of the world,' he concluded more philosophically than she'd have expected. 'The system we use now is the one I created. I put like with like. See here,' he took her elbow to steer her. 'All the umbrellas – one of the most frequently lost possessions.'

Natalia looked at them, a cascade of colours from black to orange to those with outlandish patterns, from peacock feathers to leopard-skin spots. There were telescopic ones, tiny plastic ones for children, and then the mighty, majestic black ones associated with the City gent, with steel tips and curved wooden handles. The City gentleman in bowler hat and pinstriped suit forever associated with London and immortalised in countless films. But a dying breed, she thought, as she'd not seen one in the six months she'd lived in London.

'You want handbags?' Cliff brought Natalia back to the present. 'Every size and colour and material. But not suitcases or large bags, no, they go elsewhere. As for books, they're the most frequently lost item.' He led her around a corner, then a second and a third, talking all the while.

Natalia felt a tiny flicker of anxiety at being so far away from the safety of the outer office. She had experienced his sarcastic comments and his sudden changes of mood, and now this mellower one. How safe was she? But for now his tone was pure enthusiasm. And she was enjoying having a chance to study the vault properly, the hub of all their work. So she allowed herself to be carried along, while staying on full alert.

She gazed around in continuing wonderment. So many endless ranks of shelving carrying the detritus of so many human lives. What stories these objects might tell. Their very silence and dignity seemed to say that they were not lost or misplaced, no, it was their owners who had been mislaid for a short while.

She walked around another corner and almost ran into Cliff's back. He was waiting for her. He said nothing, just waited for her reaction with a look of satisfaction on his face. The shelves were a kaleidoscope of colour so bright that at first she couldn't work out what it all was. After she'd adjusted to the dazzle, she gasped. 'It's children's school boxes, and pencil cases. Oh and lunchboxes, too!' she said, trying to move backwards slightly, as she felt trapped between Cliff and the shelving.

'Children – they'd forget their heads if they weren't screwed on. But so do their parents. See here.'

Cliff wanted her to continue following him deeper into the vault. She wondered whether she was right to do so. Was she being lulled into a false sense of security? When might she safely say she wanted to turn back without seeming rude? Great Uncle Jan had been prickly and very easily offended. Natalia recalled the time when he'd given his neighbour plants and vegetables from his garden. When the neighbour had a close family party and didn't invite him, he never spoke to them again.

She chose to venture a few more yards, and was rewarded with the sight of an endless ocean of push-chairs. 'Now how do you mislay one of these?' Cliff asked. 'They're one of the least-claimed items. Not much we can do wi' them but hand them over to charity once the three months holding period is up.' He reached out and pressed some light switches on the wall. As overhead lighting hummed on, she saw the vault stretched away even further, much further than she'd ever have believed was possible.

Natalia decided that this was as far as she wanted to go. She stood her ground and looked around. Her curiosity was aroused by a plain door set into the wall. It did not have a sign on it.

'Where does that door go to? Is it a way out?' she asked.

Cliff suddenly began to shift his weight. 'That room's off-limits. Need special permission to go in there. I keep it locked at all times. Special Items only.'

He took a step away, but she refused to move.

'Special Items? Do you mean very valuable items, like cameras or jewellery?'

'Well, those are kept under lock and key, but not in there.' Cliff was not going to reveal more. 'Now look over here, isn't it a shame that people manage to mislay their false limbs.'

Natalia allowed herself to be distracted, but her curiosity was still piqued. She would like to know what was so special about that room. Maybe Cliff had a little kitchen in there, a home from home! Her eyes strayed over the prosthetic limbs, onto the next shelf – and then she saw it. Her heart hammering, she clutched at Cliff's sleeve. 'Oh look, look there. I don't believe it. Can I see that scarf please?'

5

It was on the topmost rack. Some sixth sense must have guided her to it. Or perhaps it was the colours that had attracted her, the oranges and yellows glowing gently. It was Helen Bookman's scarf. Or, if not hers, then one exactly like it.

'That scarf, would you reach it down for me please?'

Cliff, she was pleased to note, did not question her request. He immediately sprang into action. He fetched some steps, climbed up and handed down the scarf to her.

'This scarf looks familiar,' he said. 'Why is that?'

'You were looking at the poster a short

while ago pinned upon the noticeboard. I put it there. The woman in the photograph, the missing woman, is wearing a scarf just like this one.'

'Aye, I can see that now. Do you know the woman?'

'No, but I met her husband, Peter Bookman, this morning at Baker Street station. Poor man, he was in a terrible state. I promised to help him, so I put up the picture of his wife in our office.' The scarf felt light and luxurious in her hands. It was woven from silk and very fine wool.

'If that's her scarf, it could help her husband?'

'We can check the computer records to see when it was found and where it was handed in.' Natalia looked up at him hopefully. 'Do you have to leave now?'

Cliff looked at her for a moment and came to a decision. 'I'm OK for another ten minutes. We can use the terminal at my desk and tap into Sherlock from there.'

Despite the fact that Cliff was helping her and that he had not done anything out of the ordinary, Natalia still felt a sense of relief as they approached his control desk, near the entrance to the vault. Cliff entered his password, using two stubby fingers, and then laboriously started to key in the tag number.

'Let me,' Natalia suggested. 'I'm faster.'

He stood back and let her sit down. She was conscious of him standing right behind her, watching her every move. She quickly went through the sequences that would lead her to the scarf. She hoped that whoever had logged it in would have given as much detail as possible. The training officer had said that filling in all the boxes was not essential, but could be helpful. She could now see why.

Up came the file. There was a thumbnail photo of the scarf. As she read on, her scalp began to tingle.

'Date handed in – two days ago. Date it reached us – yesterday. That would fit,' she said. 'Helen disappeared last Friday, her husband says, and today is Tuesday.' She knew, though, that it sometimes took up to ten days for a lost item to reach the LPO.

'Possibly,' he agreed.

Natalia scrolled down. 'Found on a west-bound Circle Line and handed in at High Street Kensington – that means she was travelling from the direction of Victoria towards Paddington, probably. If it *is* her scarf, then maybe it will help us find out where she was going, or coming from. And – oh my goodness, look here! The box for pos-sible related items has been checked – that means other items found in the same place, I think!' Her nimble fingers moved over the keyboard as she searched the screen, picking out every detail. 'OK if I search on?'

She heard Cliff draw in a breath and looked up at him. He seemed to be looking into the distance, considering, then he looked at her.

'I really should lock up but ... very well,' he relented. 'I'll give you another few minutes. I'll start my security rounds now.' Then he walked off.

In the sudden quiet, Natalia noticed for the first time how his thick-soled working boots, which he kept highly polished, made no sound at all. Not even a squeak of leather. No wonder he'd been able to creep up on her and Rasheda. And he must know this building inside-out, as he'd worked there for twenty years; he'd know every short cut, every nook and every cranny. She supposed it was natural he would be reluctant to let her continue. Even if he had no other commitment, he'd be wanting his supper. As if in sympathy, her stomach growled.

Natalia continued typing, tucking away in her mind the other piece of information she'd seen. The operative who'd logged in the scarf and related items was none other than Avon Gould.

Up came the next file. A pair of shoes. Stylish tan leather, two-inch heels, with chain detail over the top. Make: Dolce & Gabbana. Size seven. She blessed Avon for her devotion to shoes and giving all that detail. Size seven. She felt she was beginning to get a picture of Helen. She could be quite tall, with feet that size, as tall as her husband, and the shoes were a narrow cut, so she had slender feet. She imagined that Helen would have made heads turn when she entered a room, with her individual fashion sense, abundantly curling hair, and height.

It was her forlorn expression though, Natalia mused, that did not fit that picture of a well-groomed, confident woman. As she'd seen with her husband Peter today, the outer picture presented by clothes and hair and accent were at odds with their inner selves.

A scarf and a pair of shoes, lost or mislaid together. Losing clothing such as a scarf, hat or gloves was easily done. But a pair of shoes? Perhaps she'd been taking them to the cobbler's for repair.

The third and final item popped up, and as it did so Natalia felt a mix of concern and hope in equal measures. It was a handbag. A woman's most treasured and essential companion. What could make her part company with her handbag. Was she the victim of a mugging? If her money and credit cards were gone, that could be very informative.

Natalia made a note of the LPO's tag numbers and jumped up. 'Cliff, Cliff!' she called out.

'Yes?' he said from behind her and she whirled round. He'd managed to sneak upon her again in those noiseless shoes. She felt a shiver of apprehension. She wondered if he got some sort of pleasure out of sneaking up on people.

'There's a handbag and a pair of shoes. Have we time to fetch them now? If this poor woman has had an accident or been attacked, anything we can do might help find her.'

She held out the piece of paper on which she'd noted the handbag tag number, keeping her hand from trembling. That section was deepest into the vault. She would go to the nearby shoe section. Not only was she already familiar with it from earlier that day, but she would feel more secure.

She waited for him to object or insist they call senior management for authorisation.

'Give me both, this is where I'll be quicker,' was all he said resignedly.

While she printed off the details of the bag, shoes and scarf, then shut down the computer, she could hear faint movement in the far reaches of the vault; the scraping of ladders, a rattle of shelves. Then there was silence. She looked up. Some of the lights had been switched off already and she was looking towards darkness. In the outer office, the cheerful chatter and clatter of the cleaners had long gone. All she could hear was the slow tick of the clock on the wall, and the central heating cooling down.

'Cliff!' she said loudly, 'Are you there? Are you all right?'

Suddenly he appeared from a side alley. His expression was thunderous. 'I couldna find a thing,' he grated. 'I searched, but the shoes and handbag are nowhere to be seen. Stefan will have a few questions to answer when he comes in tomorrow.' Natalia opened her mouth, ready to defend her friend, but there was no need as Cliff went on, 'He's a reliable lad. He might know something to help you.' Natalia felt relieved. So he did have respect for his young assistant after all.

'The shoes are perhaps not so important. But the handbag, that is a blow. It could have held clues – a train ticket, something like that.'

'I've never had an item go missing under my watch, not until the Hoaxer. And now this! I'll turn the vault upside-down tomorrow, if I have to. There's no way they could have walked.'

Cliff left her to continue his locking-up circuit. Natalia was relieved to be no longer the main focus of his attention. She went into the main office. Peter Bookman. She must ring him immediately and let him know what she'd discovered. He would be able to identify the objects from the thumbnail photographs.

She switched on her mobile and saw she had three texts and a voice mail, all from

Dermot, starting with 'R U working late?', to a voice mail 'Where are you, are you all right?' She quickly texted him 'Sry Sry, leaving now! Xxx'. Then, she went over to the noticeboard and, reading the number from the poster, dialled Peter Bookman's mobile. She reached his voice mail.

'Hello,' she said awkwardly. 'We met at Baker Street station this morning. I took your poster. I work at the Lost Property Office. A scarf like your wife's has been handed in. Also maybe shoes and handbag. We are looking for these but I have photos.' She didn't want to tell him they'd been lost while in the LPO's care, especially as she was sure Cliff and Stefan would find them in the morning. 'They were handed in at High Street Kensington station yesterday morning, found on Circle Line westbound.' She gave her contact details and then rang off.

She'd been walking through reception as she talked. Outside, she looked up at the ornate and elegant mansion blocks above the LPO office and Baker Street station. No one would have thought that below them was the hidden world she'd just been viewing.

Cliff now caught up with her. She waited while he secured the front door, shivering slightly in the cool night air, and feeling disoriented at being back in the real world of a London night again.

'Good night, Cliff,' she said. 'Thank you

for your help. Are you going home now?'

A slightly shifty look came into his eyes. 'I've something to do first. You?'

'Yes, Dermot is waiting for me to have supper.'

'Very well. See you tomorrow.' He started off, then said over his shoulder, 'Maybe, I mean. Good luck with Omar. You'll need it.'

Natalia stared after his fast-retreating back, as he reached into his coat pocket for something. It seemed as if he suddenly couldn't wait to get away from her. Was that because he felt guilty about the missing handbag? Or to avoid her questioning him more closely about his evening activities? Perhaps he was only pretending he had something to do, somewhere to be, but was actually going home to an empty home and a lonely TV supper for one. She had heard that he wasn't married, and he had never mentioned a partner of any kind. But she resolved not to lower her guard or her suspicions yet, where Cliff was concerned. However many Great Uncles he reminded her of, or lonely TV suppers he might eat.

6

'I think I should be jealous of this Cliff McDougall, so I should,' Dermot teased, scooping a big helping of chicken chow mein onto each of their plates, and just catching a slippery noodle before it slithered to the floor. 'Inviting you alone into his lair and sweet talking you with tales of false teeth and umbrellas.' He suddenly nuzzled Natalia's neck. She squealed and laughed and pushed him away.

'It wasn't like that,' she protested. 'We were looking for the lost woman's things – oh, where's the soy sauce gone?' she said in Polish, hunting in a cupboard and finally locating it behind a tin of beans.

'He must have had some reason for inviting you in there in the first place though. You said he never spoke with you before.'

Natalia shook soy sauce onto her helping of beef in oyster sauce – they usually shared two choices – then handed the bottle to Dermot. 'Yes, well ... he thinks I work hard. He respects people who are serious about their work.'

'You do, too. Too damn hard. And he'd better respect my woman if he's taking her into dark corners, or he'll have me to deal with! Come on with you, I've got some beers in the fridge, we'll take them next door and settle in front of the TV.'

Tonight had been Dermot's turn to cook. As they both worked long hours, and both had long journeys to work, in opposite directions, it seemed natural to them to take it in turns to get supper during the week. Dermot usually bought in a takeaway. And he usually remembered Natalia's favourite dishes, too. Her stomach rumbled as she sat down and waited while Dermot poured them both some beer. Polish beer, from a specialist supermarket not too far away.

'Anyway, how come this woman was lost in your property office?' Dermot said as they started to eat with relish.

'You!' Natalia said, punching him lightly on the arm. 'She wasn't lost in there. She went missing on the Circle Line.'

'It's known for it. Many, many people have got on the Circle Line, never to be seen again – it takes forever to get anywhere.'

'True.' Natalia nodded. When they'd been looking for a flat to buy, they'd spent much time criss-crossing London in their hunt, and the worst delays always seemed to be on the Circle or the District Lines. At first she thought she'd never get used to the complicated network of lines that rumbled beneath the busy streets of the British capital above.

But gradually she developed a fascination for the different coloured lines, and joined her fellow Londoners in their daily battle of wits to make the system work for them. And passing through Baker Street every day was an added bonus, being the oldest underground station in the world.

'And here we are living in Hackney, with its reputation as one of the roughest neighbourhoods in London, and for its special line in lap-dancing clubs, having to use the overground train before we even get to an interchange and go underground.'

'But at least we have two bedrooms,' she reminded him, as they settled into their usual argument on the subject. 'We couldn't have afforded a flat this size anywhere else.'

'I know, I know. It was Hackney or a cardboard box on the M25, so you keep reminding me. I'm still not sure which is the most dangerous place to live,' he sighed. 'When I think of that lovely flat in Crouch End—'

'It's not *that* dangerous in Hackney! It's an up-and-coming area, I was reading in the *Standard* last week.'

'So they keep telling us. Then this place will be worth a mint. But when? Will we be retired by then?' Dermot relented and reached over to squeeze her hand. 'I wasn't having a go at you. Fancy another beer? I'll go and fetch it.' He liked his beer very cold, straight from the fridge, and he was not fond of Guinness. Natalia teased him that he was not a true Irishman.

While he was gone Natalia looked round their living room.

Their apartment was on the fourth floor of a new block of flats. Everything was fresh and new, painted white and cream, with floor-to-ceiling windows and small balcony looking out over a green. She loved the newness of it, despite the compact galley kitchen. Back in Poland, her parents' home was old and shabby and crowded. Goodness knows how Dermot, who'd been boarding with them while he worked on a local construction site, ever found room to romance her.

'How was your day?' she asked Dermot when he returned.

'Oh sure, it's all going fine. We had to call the police and fire brigade when one of the boys thought he saw an unexploded bomb from the Second World War.'

'No!'

'Turned out to be a rusty old tin bath buried upside down, but the police made us wait till they were sure. We all had a bit of a laugh and a crack about that. At this rate England'll be hosting the Olympics in 3012.' As a building contractor, Dermot had contracts preparing land and building arenas out in London's Dockland and East

End for the 2012 Olympics.

'You're not seriously worried about falling behind schedule, are you?' The pressure to deliver on time and within budget was immense.

'No, we'll be all right. It's just everyone else who's not reaching their targets.'

Natalia knew that behind Dermot's joking exterior, he did worry about meeting deadlines. Everything he did, he poured himself into with passion. She knew he needed time to unwind in the evenings, or he'd be so revved up he'd never be able to sleep.

'This missing woman now,' he said thoughtfully, as he collected their empty plates together. 'That's right up your street, isn't it? Finding people.'

She gave him a grateful smile. She didn't know whether Avon or Donna had read or remembered, from her personnel file, her previous employment. She'd worked for an agency that helped people track down the parent who had given them up for adoption. She'd found a deep satisfaction in the tracing process. It was Dermot who'd spotted the advert for the job at the Lost Property Office and persuaded her to try for it. Once again she was able to make those connections.

'Her husband seemed to be at the end of his rope.'

'Tether,' Dermot corrected automatically.

'Yes, and he said the police are not listening to him. He said they don't care. I suppose they must think she has left him.'

'Strange, though, her scarf, bag and shoes all turning up together like that. If they *are* hers.'

'He will be able to identify them. I don't know what to make of it yet, but I will puzzle it out.'

'OK. Which one are you, Detective Cagney or Lacey?

'Do I look like either of them?'

'Ah, you put them both in the shade.'

She stuck her tongue out at him. 'Go and get our dessert.'

Natalia drank the last of her beer, and half watched the nature documentary on the television. She was surprised Peter Bookman had not called her back yet, but perhaps it was just as well. Surely tomorrow they would find the shoes and handbag.

Their landline ringing broke into her thoughts. 'Can you answer that?' Dermot called from the kitchen. 'I can't get this damned ice cream out!'

'Hello,' Natalia answered the phone, hoping to hear Peter's voice.

'Is my dad there?' It was Nuala, Dermot's twelve-year-old daughter.

'He's just in the kitchen. How are you, Nuala?'

'OK.' There was a sigh. 'Can I talk to him now?'

'I'll take the phone to him. You're coming over this week, aren't you?'

'Yeah.'

Natalia contented herself with that and passed the phone to Dermot. 'Nuala,' she mouthed.

'Hi, darlin'. What's up?' He took the phone and raised his brows at Natalia, who nodded. He gave her a quick kiss then went to the tiny box room, which was his study-cum-workroom and also his son, Connor's, bedroom when he stayed over, the second bedroom being Nuala's. Natalia had suggested he take calls from his children in there so they felt they had his full attention and knew she was not listening in.

She put the two plates of fruit and ice cream in the fridge, then began to empty the dishwasher, ready to re-load it. As she did so, she glanced at the photos stuck on the kitchen noticeboard. Dermot's son, nine-year-old Connor, grinned widely, showing the gap where he'd lost a tooth skateboarding. He had straight, fair hair, teased up into spikes, and guileless, china-blue eyes. He looked just like his mother, Kathleen.

Beside him, Nuala scowled. Her thick, black hair threatened to be as curly as her dad's, so she spent a lot of time with ceramic hair straighteners. Her dark-blue eyes, the same colour as his, hid her true feelings. She wore tight blue jeans, a skimpy top and a wide belt. Another photo showed Connor and Nuala sitting either side of their dad. Natalia had taken it when they'd first moved in. She knew she'd twisted Dermot's arm to move to an area he wasn't keen on, but this way, being able to afford two bedrooms and a boxroom, both Nuala and Connor could have their own space, somewhere to keep clothes and other possessions.

Dermot had an arm around each child. Nuala was grimacing and crossing her eyes, while Connor was sticking out his tongue. Natalia smiled fondly at the memory. She felt she knew where she was with Connor. He just wanted to copy his dad, play sports with him, and accepted Natalia as not only a provider of food, but also as someone who made his dad happy.

Nuala was another matter. Sometimes she would chatter away about school or her friends. Other times she'd sit sullenly in a chair, iPod screwed in her ears, texting for all she was worth, shutting out all attempts at communication. Natalia sensed she was a troubled girl and she waited, hoping that the troubles would pass as normal teenage sulks, or that Nuala would eventually reveal herself. She tolerated Natalia, that was all.

Dishwasher filled, Natalia ran warm water into the washing-up bowl for their glasses. 'One day,' she said to herself, nodding at Nuala. She didn't want to rival or replace their mother, but hoped to forge some kind of good relationship with Dermot's children.

She smiled wistfully. That was genuinely what she wanted but she had to admit that a tiny corner of her mind had fantasised that, while Dermot was busy playing computer games with, or teaching the finer points of fantasy football to Connor, she would have girly time with Nuala. Or while Dermot watched films and talked with his daughter, she would have fun playing board games with his son. It hadn't happened yet, and might never. However, it was early days still. She'd only known them for six months now, ever since she'd come to join Dermot in London.

How she'd missed him in the time they were apart! They'd met when Dermot had come from Dublin to work in Poland. He'd been filled with hot rage at the way his ex-wife had taken their children to live in London when she'd been offered a good job there, without caring whether he'd be able to visit or have access. Rage masking his grief, he'd decided that the best way to avoid pain was not to see them at all, so he'd taken a contracting job in Poland.

Natalia had wondered how Dermot's ex-wife could have simply taken the children off like that. Had it been some kind of revenge for perceived wrongs? But, since meeting her, she'd discovered she was just a woman who acted on impulse and thought afterwards, careless of other people's feelings.

Gradually, Natalia's family's warmth had calmed him down and they had fallen in love. She knew she'd like to use her skills to reconnect him with his children. Pride held him back for some time. Then the Olympics programme offered him the perfect opportunity to come to London and start afresh.

'God, you're beautiful, my own personal witchy woman.' She hadn't heard him come in. He called her witchy woman because of her clear, green eyes. He put his arms round her from behind and pulled her against him. 'Thanks,' he murmured into her hair. 'Still no wiser about what's bugging her, but she sounded more cheerful when I said good night.' He turned her round and kissed her. 'How about it, Natalia? How about having one of these maddening children of our own.' She met his eyes then looked away, as pain shafted through her heart. 'Maybe,' she said. 'Maybe one day but ... not now. I'm not ready.'

'OK. OK, darlin'.' He held her tight in understanding then let her go. 'Now, where's that ice cream?'

7

The journey to work the next day was the usual complex fight against London's creaky underground system. A suspect package at King's Cross disrupted the Hammersmith and City Line, while signalling problems at Hainault meant the Central Line was only running westbound. 'We have a good service on all other lines,' the public announcement system reassured in its regular update. The only trouble was, they then had to absorb all the extra passengers.

Natalia zigzagged her way along, finding herself standing dangerously close to the platform edges as more commuters packed their way in, watching the mice who lived under the rails scurrying around searching for crumbs, and then feeling the warm rush of air as a train approached. She shoved her way into trains, like a practised Londoner, holding her head back so the doors could close, and then stood sandwiched between other commuters who endured the journey by reading newspapers or books, or listening to their iPods. Tubes at this time of day tended to be quiet. Apart from the occasional sigh or grumble when the train stopped in a tunnel for what seemed like no reason, no one spoke. Sometimes the driver would apologise for the wait, promising to get under way as soon as the next station was cleared, or a signal turned from red to green.

As soon as she reached the surface at Baker Street, Natalia looked at her mobile. She had not yet received a reply from Peter Bookman, and she saw now that he still had not contacted her. She thought this was odd. She had expected him to be in touch immediately. She supposed there could be many explanations. He could have been taken ill. Maybe he'd forgotten to charge up his mobile, and stayed with family instead of going home. Yet wouldn't he be checking his phone all the time, in case his wife called?

'What's new?' Homeless Joe was in his usual pitch. She gave him a coin, as she did every day, wishing she had time to stop and talk, to find out why he'd ended up on the streets. He cracked his usual crooked smile. 'Found the lost woman yet?'

He'd remembered! 'I've found some of her belongings.'

'You'll do it. Keep looking! Someone's got to care.' Homeless Joe waved and then tucked the coin away. He always wore the same clothes. On top was what had once been a smart, navy overcoat, several sizes too big, and underneath were several layers of jumpers and T-shirts, while on his feet some filthy trainers that were coming apart at the soles. She couldn't tell how old he was but the hair that stuck out from under his woolly pompom hat was jet black.

Uplifted by this encounter after the nightmare journey, Natalia hurried up Baker Street to the office. There was thin, winter sunshine this morning and she had a glimpse of pale-blue sky above the tall buildings either side of the road.

Mark was at the reception desk, looking at the computer terminal there. 'Hi, Natalia,' he said breezily when he saw her.

'Hi, Mark. How was the football last night?'

His face lit up. 'Brilliant! Great game! We won! There was a penalty shoot out that went in our favour and... I guess that's enough information!'

'I understand the offside rule. Now my husband's son, Connor, is trying to get me to go to a live game. Are you on reception today?'

'Oh no, I was just looking for something.' He didn't meet her eyes, and started typing at the keyboard.

'OK, I go on.' She was almost inside the main office when Mark called after her, 'Your friend's waiting for you at your desk. He said you were expecting him.'

A friend? A male friend? Natalia hurried across the room. At first all she could see was the bowed, dark head of a man sitting in her chair. Then, as she approached, he lifted his face and stared at her. It was Peter Bookman in person! His red-rimmed eyes had dark shadows under them and, although he'd made an attempt to shave, it had not been entirely successful, and he'd cut himself, too. But there was something different about him today. He was not so defeated. Instead he had an almost feverish intensity.

'Mrs O'Shea? It's Peter Bookman,' he said, standing up.

'Natalia, please. How are you?' she said in confusion, shaking his hand. His palm was cold and hard. 'I'm sorry, that's a silly question.'

'No, thank you for asking. When I got your message last night I went straight to the police station to pass on the information you gave me.'

'Was it helpful?'

He gave a harsh laugh. 'They decided to interview me. Again. Wanted to go over every detail. Don't get me wrong. I'd tell the story over and over ad infinitum if I felt it would help. But I had the strong impression they were just going through the motions to keep me quiet and get me off their backs.'

'I'm sorry. I expect they have many things to deal with.'

'I may be just a statistic to them, but this is my life, and it's falling apart!' He banged his fist on her desk.

Natalia took a step backwards. 'You're feeling very upset, it's understandable,' she said more formally. 'Can I get you something to drink? We have a machine, it's quick and quite good.'

He quietened. 'Tea, yes, tea please. I've drunk so much coffee–'

'Please sit down. I'll get another chair in a moment.'

To her relief, he was seated when she returned, in a chair he'd fetched himself. He'd taken off his coat and hung it over the back. He wore a pale-grey suit, white shirt and pink tie. On closer examination, she saw the shirt had not been ironed and there was a stain on the suit lapel. He saw her examining him, and thought she was admiring his tie. 'Helen bought this for me. When I wear it, I feel close to her.' He gave a bitter laugh. 'I suppose I sound like a fool.'

'The police were unsympathetic, you say.' Natalia handed him his tea and sat down.

'Went through every minute fact again. Not that I mind, if it'll help find Helen, or make them start *doing* something. I suppose it would make things easier if I knew something, but I don't. I wish I did.' He stopped and took a sip of tea.

'What happened last Friday?'

Peter Bookman sighed. 'I left for work at half-past seven as usual, to get from Swiss

Cottage where we live, to Canary Wharf where we both work. Helen usually comes with me but she was having a flexi-time day, working at home. The next thing I knew was when Helen's mother called me. She'd spoken to Helen about nine a.m., at home, and arranged to go over in the afternoon but, when she arrived, Helen wasn't there. She tried calling her mobile, no reply, waited a while, then called me in case I knew if Helen had changed her plans. I told her she hadn't spoken a word to me.

'There was no sign of a disturbance at our flat, and she'd locked up and put the answer machine on. I think that's why the police think she decided to leave me. But why? Since then–' His voice broke.

'The anxiety must be terrible for you, and for Helen's mother. You must both be exhausted.'

'The police didn't let me go till after midnight, and anyway, I haven't really been sleeping.' He took another drink of tea, then sat up straighter and gave her a searching look. 'You've found some of Helen's belongings. That's why I've come. Where are they?'

'I think this is hers.' Natalia opened the bottom drawer of her desk and took out the scarf. Once again she was struck by the richness of the colours and texture of the material.

Peter Bookman snatched it from her hand and immediately held it to his nose. His eyes closed in near ecstasy. 'Yes, it's hers,' he murmured. 'That's her perfume. I buy it for her every Christmas.' He opened his eyes and she saw they were still bloodshot. 'Can you smell it?'

Natalia sniffed gently. 'Yes! So you think this is Helen's?'

He looked at the label, held it up. 'I'm almost one hundred per cent certain. We bought it last year, when we went to Morocco. Helen was doing research for a painting. She paints, you know, in her spare time. She's very talented.' A fond light came into his eyes. 'We had a wonderful time there.' He leaned forward eagerly, trying to see into her drawer. 'And the handbag, her shoes? They will confirm it.'

Natalia nudged the drawer shut with her foot. 'Let me show you the log-in details. I have photographs here. We will need to ask for as much proof as possible, for identification purposes, as we always do, but in the circumstances–'

But Peter Bookman wasn't listening to her. He reached down to pull the drawer handle open again, as Natalia tried to hold it closed. After a brief tussle, he won, the drawer came open and he saw it was empty. He jumped to his feet, all semblance of calm gone. 'Where are her other things? What are you not telling me? What are you keeping from me?'

'Nothing, I assure you, Peter.'

He loomed over her, then collapsed back into his chair and rubbed a hand wearily across his face. 'I'd begun to hope that maybe there would be something in her handbag that would give me a clue as to where she'd gone or why. Who am I kidding? This is hopeless.'

Natalia drank her tea, waited a moment for him to collect himself, then said, 'Please look at these photographs and descriptions. The bag and shoes were found with the scarf.'

Peter stared at the print-outs almost as if he could not take them in. Then he took a deep breath and drew them closer. 'Yes,' he confirmed, excitement returning. 'Those are like a pair of shoes she wore, as far as I recall. But the handbag is definitely hers. It's a Mulberry.'

'How can you be so sure?'

'We were together when she chose it.' He gave a small smile of reminiscence. 'It was only a couple of months ago. Took her forever to make up her mind. I was feeling impatient, angry even. If only I hadn't–' He buried his face in his hands.

'If only you hadn't what?' Natalia prompted.

He looked up. 'It's the feeling of guilt,' he

said in a low voice. 'You go over everything that you've said, wonder if there was something you should have done ... whether you drove her away? And then I think, no, Helen would have talked to me. We always talked. Or so I thought.' He paused. 'I almost *want* it to be that she's left me, even though I don't know why, than that something worse has happened.' He sat quietly for a moment, lost in thought, then squared his shoulders. 'What do I have to do now? What sort of proof should I bring, and do I need to sign some forms?'

'I'm sorry, Peter, we haven't located the other items in the vault yet. We are looking for them this morning.'

'What?' Peter's voice went up with incredulity. 'Are you telling me the Lost Property Office has *lost* my wife's things?'

'No, I'm saying we are looking for them,' she tried to reassure him.

'Have you any idea what I'm going through? You get my hopes up, and now this.'

'I promise I'll call you as soon as they're found.'

'You promise. You promise. And you expect me to trust that? The Lost Property Office LOST my wife's things–'

'Everything all right, Natalia? I heard voices.'

Stefan was beside her. She stood up. 'Stefan, this is Peter Bookman. Has Cliff mentioned the handbag and shoes?'

'Oh yes, we're searching now, this minute, Mr Bookman.'

Peter Bookman hesitated, looking from one to the other of them and back again. 'Of course,' he said, suddenly deflated, packing the scarf in his briefcase, then picking it and his coat up. 'I should be thanking you for everything you've done, Natalia. Forgive me. I don't know what came over me. Promise you'll call me the second they turn up?'

'Promise.'

'This way, Mr Bookman.' Stefan indicated the way out and escorted him across the office as far as reception.

Natalia drew in a deep breath. The poor man was in an even worse state than yesterday. She decided to excuse his aggressive behaviour and give him the benefit of the doubt. It was pressure and fear that had made him blow up like that. The not knowing was the worst, she understood that. Not knowing whether Helen had chosen to go and was safe, or was lying injured, or worse. The not knowing. Her mind filled with unwanted images from the past. If only she knew, could be sure–

'He's gone now, Natalia.' Stefan was beside her again. He laid a reassuring hand briefly on her shoulder and she caught a faint whiff of fresh, sweet tobacco smoke from him.

'Thanks, Stefan. I don't think Peter has

slept since his wife disappeared. His mind must be full of weird fancies right now.'

'Cliff told me about the shoes and the handbag. I hope we find them soon. If Avon doesn't slow us down. New security, she says.' He rolled his eyes.

Natalia smiled gratefully at her friend, who looked as fresh and fit as always, whatever he'd been up to the night before. She watched as he headed towards the vault. She saw that Mark had returned from reception. He chased after Stefan and caught hold of his arm, and held out the file the two young men had been studying the day before. But Stefan shook his head and refused to take it, so Mark shrugged and went back to his desk, with a quick look towards Avon and Donna to make sure they hadn't observed him.

Natalia smiled to herself. Those two young men were always up to something, especially Mark. But she was grateful for that moment of everyday normality to enable her to recover from the encounter with Peter Bookman, which had shaken her. Then she recollected that she should be joining Omar downstairs in the CCTV room, and quickly picked up what she needed and headed for the back stairs.

8

The air in the stairwell to the basement was cool. At the bottom of the stairs, a corridor disappeared into darkness. There was just one door set into the wall opposite, with a frosted-glass window in it, and there was a light on inside. Natalia paused outside the CCTV room, holding the door handle, when it was tugged open from inside, knocking her off balance.

Omar's tall frame filled the doorway. 'So glad you could make it. Are you coming in?' His tone was sardonic.

'Yes, of course. I'm sorry I'm late. I had a meeting.'

'Time is of no consequence here,' he said, standing aside and ushering her into a drab, dingy room, which seemed to be a grave-yard for old desks and broken chairs. There were no pictures, no calendars, nothing to brighten the walls. He had set up two desks and viewing screens in the middle of the dull-brown carpet, facing away from each other.

'Sit here,' Omar said, coolly. 'It's Mrs O'Shea, isn't it?'

She nodded. 'Natalia,' she said and held

out her hand. Omar hesitated, then took it in a brief handshake. His long fingers were warm and dry. He wasn't hostile, but he wasn't friendly either.

'If you want coffee, there is a kettle.' He pointed to the floor on one side. A kettle, mugs, coffee jar and a bottle of milk stood ready. 'I will show you how to operate the screen and the basics of how to interpret what you see. However, it is not something everyone can master, and those who can take a while to refine their skills.'

'How long does it take to train?'

'According to Ms Avon and Ms Donna, about five minutes,' he said caustically. 'In reality, some months, more. Most can master the basics eventually. Only some have a real aptitude for this kind of focussed observation.'

Although he was being punctiliously polite, he was also keeping her at arm's length. He would not bestow his confidence lightly, after the treatment he'd received. But from his attitude to Avon and Donna, Natalia deduced that she was tainted by association with them. For all Omar knew, she might have been sent to spy on him!

'I do have a description of your shoe fetishist for you.'

'You do?'

'Look for a figure clad head to toe in black.'

'Huh?'

'She – or he – is always in a burqa. That's why it has been impossible to identify them. But your Avon seems convinced that it shouldn't be too difficult to zoom in on the culprit – in a city where 8.5% of the population is Muslim. But, hey, it's already looking good. Only half of them are women, and only a small percentage of them wear traditional garb. Ah, but then I didn't take into account all the tourists. But no, if Avon says it can be done, then who am I to caution. So, go ahead, make yourself comfortable. You may be here a while.'

Natalia sat in the hard, plastic chair at her new desk and waited while Omar began to set up her machine. If he was the CCTV genius she'd been told, she could see why he would be furious at being sidelined to such a grim backwater. As Rasheda had said, it was yet another humiliation. In which case, why didn't he simply find another job and leave? What reason could he have for staying and putting up with this unfair treatment? Surely it had to be more than a matter of pride.

She glanced over at his desk, and saw he'd personalised it with photographs. One was of himself in younger days, laughing together with some other young man, arms around each other's shoulders. In the background across rocky, sandy terrain were the square white and fawn houses of a desert town, the tops of palm trees just visible over flat roofs.

The other was of a woman in a hijab, her hair hidden under the pink scarf, smiling into the camera. Two small children with solemn faces sat beside her on a sofa, between them a baby. Omar saw her gaze. 'My wife Jamila and our children,' he said. 'Two boys and a girl.'

'Are they at school yet?'

'No, the eldest goes next year.'

'My husband has two children from his first marriage. Nuala is twelve but thinks she is fourteen, and Connor is nine,' she found herself telling him, with a sense of disloyalty at what she had omitted. Omar's dark gaze rested on her momentarily but he did not soften. 'I see,' he said, then went on briskly. 'Now let me show you how to examine the screen.'

He gave her some instruction, but she could tell he was only giving her the bare minimum. Perhaps he saw no point as she could be ordered upstairs again at a moment's notice. He was subject to other people's whims, not in command of his own destiny.

'How far back do these tapes go that we have here?' she asked.

'One month. You are to look at the area associated with this building and its surroundings.'

'Yes. Donna and Avon want to find out who our hoaxer is.'

Omar's shrug told her that he considered this of no importance at all. 'Today your hoaxer, tomorrow the Shoe Fetishist, what will it be the next? There are bigger issues out there in the world. But your Avon doesn't see this.' There was contempt in his voice.

'May I also look at other tapes?' Natalia asked. 'For example the Circle Line last Friday?'

Omar shrugged again. 'Why not? But you had better look for your hoaxer first. Perhaps you, a beginner, will find in ten minutes what the rest of us trained idiots have failed to see.'

Ouch, thought Natalia, making herself a coffee. He is not a happy man and who can blame him? It was a shame that he seemed to have given up and stopped trying, however, and no longer cared about his work. Perhaps he really was deliberately trying to sabotage the system.

Set back to back, so they were not distracted by each other's screen, she began to follow the jerky movements, studying each frame carefully. At first she found it impossible to work out what was happening, and to recognise individual faces as passengers and passers by moved about. She kept asking Omar questions and then, after a couple of hours, began to feel that she was getting the hang of it.

Natalia felt a surge of excitement. Perhaps now she would be able to spot something actually worth seeing. The concentration required was fierce. She coped by taking brief moments away from the screen to rest her eyes and brain, and also exercise her legs and hands. She didn't want to miss anything. She wanted to stay sharp. She was conscious of Omar's eyes on her from time to time, but he made no attempt to talk to her.

She ate a sandwich at her desk for lunch, while Omar opened up a lunchbox prepared by his wife, and then disappeared behind the *Independent* newspaper. Natalia read some more of Sherlock Holmes's adventures in *A Study In Scarlet.* Then it was back to the grainy flickering black-and-white screens again.

After a while, she began to find a rhythm in her work, even though it was very new to her. She was able to call on some of her skills from her previous career in Poland. There, she had approached each case with as open a mind as she could. Each adoptee who sought their genetic or birth parents had a different story to tell, had their own preconceptions, fears, hopes and dreams. She had to rid herself of all that, what she called 'emotional noise', and focus only on the facts.

Secondly, she had to have a dogged persistence to keep trawling through records and archives until she found some evidence, however small and insignificant it might seem. Indeed, Sherlock Holmes would be proud of her for both these methods.

Finally, she also had to allow herself occasional flashes of intuition. Guessing that a name had been misspelled, or that a town had been renamed, for example, and to follow that fresh trail.

If only it could have been as simple and straightforward as that in her own life...

It was just as she was flagging and her concentration was beginning to go, around four thirty in the afternoon, that two things happened; she saw Helen Bookman; and Stefan appeared at the door of the CCTV room, looking for her.

'Your boyfriend's here,' Omar said, jerking a thumb in Stefan's direction. Quickly, she froze the screen, and made a note of the reference number in case it didn't hold.

'Hi, Stefan, what can I do for you?'

'Come with me,' he said, and drew her outside into the echoing stairwell.

'Now Omar really will think something's going on between us! What's the secret?'

'Him? Omar, the forgotten man? You don't want to worry what he thinks, no one else does.'

'He's not so bad.' She felt compassion for Omar, despite his curtness. 'Come on, brother number one, why have you come down to see me?'

'Cliff sent me. He says he has something for you, you will know what it is.' Stefan lifted an eyebrow, but made no further comment. She was becoming aware there was a manly bond developing between him and Cliff. 'He says he will go for cigarette break. When can you meet him outside?'

Heart racing, Natalia thought for a moment. 'Tell him I'll catch him when I'm finished here, about another hour.'

Stefan nodded, blew her a kiss and was gone, his long legs taking the stairs two at a time.

The handbag! She hoped it was Helen's handbag that he'd found, not the shoes. Barely able to conceal her excitement, Natalia returned to her desk. She was aware of Omar's curious eyes on her. Let him think what he would, for now she would not confront him. But if his manner persisted in the days to come, then she would have to stand up to him.

Fingers shaking, she unfroze the screen and replayed the last segment. Yes, she was sure it was Helen Bookman. Her hair and earrings, the scarf around her neck – it had to be her. She'd studied the poster so many times she could not be mistaken. She was clutching a handrail as the train swayed. Natalia saw that, as she had surmised, she was tall and slender. She was gazing into the distance. Natalia screwed up her eyes, trying to read her expression. She seemed to be frozen, transfixed. Then, as the train stopped and other passengers got off, she took a seat at the end of the carriage beside the connecting door to the next carriage.

As Natalia watched, Helen sat with her head bent, deep in thought. Then she straightened up, as if she'd reached a decision. Almost like an automaton, she began to slide off her scarf and put it down between herself and the carriage end. She then picked up the carrier bag at her feet, took out a pair of trainers, exchanged them for her high heels and placed the heels under her scarf.

The train stopped. Helen stood up, took her carrier bag, and walked off the train. Leaving behind her scarf, shoes and handbag in a neat pile. There were only a few passengers sitting in Helen's carriage, each engrossed in a newspaper, book, or conversation. No one noticed what had taken place.

Natalia could not believe what she had just seen and replayed the sequence again and again. But it was true. Helen Bookman had quite deliberately left her belongings behind. But why? And why had she not spoken to her husband? At this point in her journey, she did not appear to be physically ill or harmed in any way.

This did not fit with the picture her husband had painted of a devoted couple, whether on holiday, out shopping together, or working in the same building and travelling to work together. Or was that the conclusion he wanted Natalia and others to reach? Yes, he seemed desperate to find out Helen's whereabouts, but were they truly a close and loving couple?

'What is it? What have you seen?' Omar's tall, spare figure appeared silently beside her. She'd been so engrossed in her own thoughts she had almost forgotten he was there, sitting behind her.

'It's incredible,' she said. 'Do you want to see?'

'You've found your hoaxer in one day?'

'No, it's something more important. You remember I wanted to look at the Circle Line tapes? Look.'

She played the sequence again, pointing out Helen on the screen.

'OK, I see a woman leaving her belongings on a train. What's the significance?'

'A woman is missing. Here, let me show you.' Natalia fetched the spare poster she carried in her bag. She unfolded it on the desk. 'Mr Bookman is desperate to find his wife,' she explained. 'Because I knew the line she was on, and the timing – we have those belongings upstairs – I was able to search in the right place. But it's so frustrating. As soon as she leaves the carriage, I lose her. I cannot find her again.'

Omar had been listening carefully. 'You really care about this woman and her husband, even though they are complete strangers. Why are you so involved with them?'

'I'm not sure. Perhaps because ... because I know what it's like to lose someone precious to you.'

He gave a slight nod, but made no further comment.

'Can I take this tape with me?'

He waved his hand, indicating yes, and turned his back on her again. Natalia began to close down and pack away her things. She had just one thought in mind. The mystery surrounding Helen's disappearance was deepening.

9

Natalia hurried up the stairs from the basement and into the main office with but one thought in her mind. Her meeting with Cliff. What was it that he wanted to give her? The excitement over finally catching a glimpse of the real, moving, albeit digital, Helen Bookman drove all other considerations from her mind.

Where was everyone? No one was at their desks. She heard a hubbub of noise and saw that everyone was gathered at the entrance to the vault. Her heart sank. What was Cliff up to now? She imagined him standing there, arms folded, bushy eyebrows beetling, refusing entry. 'Ye'll not come a step further. I'm taking over. From now on, no one goes in or out except me!'

But it wasn't Cliff guarding the entrance to the vault. It was Avon, whose Manolo Blahniked feet were planted firmly in the entranceway.

'One day,' she said. 'I've instituted this book for a single day, and already *someone* is flouting the rules.' She opened the book and ran her finger along the top of a blank page. 'It's a simple procedure. When you want to have access to the vaults, you sign your name here...' she stabbed the page with a manicured nail. 'State your purpose and the time. Then you sign out when you have finished your business.'

Natalia could imagine Avon standing in the corridors at school, ever the diligent corridor monitor, armed with a clipboard and a beady eye for those who dared to run.

'It may not seem an issue to some of you,' Avon continued, treating each of them to a frosty stare, 'but I assure you that it is of utmost importance. This hoaxer thrives on the lapses in our diligence. If we're to keep one step ahead, we must shape up! From now on, he's our number one priority...'

'How do you now it is not a woman?' asked Stefan.

Avon snapped the book shut, and everyone, Natalia included, lifted slightly onto their toes. She treated even Stefan to a frosty look.

'Thank you, Stefan,' she said, without seeming to part her teeth, a spot of red appearing on her milky-white cheek. She addressed the others again. 'The next office inspection could be any day. It will come without warning. If we're to have any chance of knocking those stooges in Manchester off the top spot, we've got to catch this hoaxer and bring him – or her – to justice.' She spoke the final word with such venom, that Natalia could envisage her stirring a cauldron in some forgotten circle of hell. Was there a place of punishment for lost-property-related offences, Natalia wondered. There would be if Avon had a say in it.

Avon's voice shook her from her musings like a cold shower.

'So, all I'm asking for is a renewed diligence in the straightforward policy.' She gave a tight-lipped smile.

'What about me and Cliff?' Stefan asked. 'Will we need our passports maybe? Or maybe have our irises scanned?'

Natalia giggled, and Avon seemed to relax

a little. Was that the trace of a sense of humour?

'Sorry, Stefan. When I said everyone, I mean *everyone*. And this is just the start. I'll be bringing more security measures in soon. That hoaxer won't be able to carry out his thieving any more. Will he ... *Mark?*'

Mark raised both palms in shock. 'Hey, why are you singling me out?'

'I have my eye on you, Mark Thomas.'

'I didn't know you cared,' Mark quipped.

'That's right,' said Avon. 'Make a joke out of it. But be warned, I have a list of suspects, and your name is near the top.'

'Yes, *kommandant*,' said Mark under his breath. Natalia caught it.

'What did you say?' said Avon.

'Look,' he replied. 'Why are you picking on me?'

'Because you haven't been doing a very good job of covering your tracks, that's why.' Avon tucked the book beneath her arm and opened her left hand. 'Visits to the vault, but not to place or fetch lost objects.' She tapped her forefinger. 'Unauthorised use of any and every computer terminal.' She tapped her second finger. 'I've seen you looking around to see if anyone's observing what you're up to. And so has Donna.' She tapped her third finger.

'That's all circumstantial,' said Mark. 'It could be anyone. It could be *you.*'

'That's enough. Just watch yourself.'

'But it wasn't me!'

'Prove it.'

Mark rolled his eyes. 'The burden of proof rests on the person making the extra-ordinary claims,' he said, with a smug smile.

Silence fell. Natalia tried to catch Cliff's eyes, but he was watching Avon with a curious mixture of affront and – could that be approbation, Natalia wondered.

'I've seen you pestering Stefan, too,' said Avon. 'Trying to get him to join in your nasty games? Why don't you own up and get it over with.'

'For the last time, because I'm innocent,' he protested. Stefan was biting his lip. He opened his mouth to speak, but Mark went on, 'You can try all you want, but I'm not owning up to something I haven't done!'

'Nonsense, you've always got a shifty look.'

'That's bullying–' Stefan began.

This was getting dangerously personal, and Natalia knew it wouldn't do any good for the office. She stepped forwards with a smile. 'I think I know where the misunder-standing is,' she said, interrupting Stefan. 'Avon, if you look in that file on Mark's desk, I think you'll find what he's been talking to Stefan about.'

Avon looked from Natalia, to Mark, then Stefan. A shiver went through her red hair.

'What are you talking about?'

'Please wait a moment.' Natalia walked over to Mark's desk, picked up the file in question, and carried it back, offering it to Avon. She opened it and began reading from a sheet of paper inside. 'Wayne Rooney, Michael Owen, Peter Crouch, Theo Walcott.' She looked up. 'What's this, the new England football team?'

'It's my dream team,' Mark said.

'Fantasy football,' Natalia said. Avon's authority visibly withered and her shoulders slumped a little. Now the drama was over, the others began drifting away up the stairs. 'Mark's a hard-working lad,' Natalia continued. 'This is how he relaxes.'

Avon looked suspiciously at both of them. 'Is this true?' she demanded. 'All that subterfuge and energy wasted on football?'

'Not *wasted*,' Mark said. 'There's money to be made. Got to get the readies to pay for the live matches. Thought Stefan might want to join in, but he decided against it.'

'So this is what you've been doing instead of working! I shall have to tell Donna.'

'Did someone say my name?' Donna's voice sounded across the room, and they saw her emerging from her office. Her hair pulled back in its customary ponytail, she looked tired at the end of a long day, with some of the polish a little worn off. Buttoning up her military-style overcoat, she paused and quipped, 'What's going on here ... planning a mutiny?'

Avon pursed her lips and held out the file as though it were the incriminating fingerprints that sewed up a murder trial.

'Mark isn't the Hoaxer,' said Avon, 'but it pains me to say he *has* been abusing company time.'

'He was only playing fantasy football,' smooth-talked Stefan.

'He was betting money!' said Avon.

'Millions all over the world play it,' said Mark now the drama was over. 'You've got to think strategy, plan tactics. It's like managing your own team.'

Donna held up her hand in a call for silence now the drama was over. 'Very well, but not on the LPO's time, OK? You're here to work, not play, hmm? Carry on, Avon. Oh, and well done.'

'Is that it?' said Avon.

'For now,' said Donna, and walked off.

She was clearly not in the mood for all this.

Avon was momentarily deflated. Certainly not the reaction she was hoping for, thought Natalia. 'You heard Donna.' Avon shoved the file back at Mark now the drama was over. 'Keep this for lunchtimes.' She thrust the signing-in book at Cliff and marched away. He grunted and placed it on the small table outside the entrance to the vault.

'Phew.' Mark ran a finger round his collar now the drama was over. 'Thank goodness for that. Thought I was going to be hauled off to Wormwood Scrubs for a second there. How did you know, Natalia?'

'I told you, my husband's been teaching his son. Mark, go carefully. Don't let the gambling get hold of you.

Mark grinned, his cheerful humour restored now the drama was over. 'I won't, I'm too mean for that. And I always hedge my bets. As you've been learning it so well, do you want to have a go?'

'Watch out!' she said, and attempted to ruffle his hair. He ducked out of the way, laughing. But Natalia's mind was only half on Mark. She was still driven by the urgency to meet with Cliff. She saw him crossing the office towards reception, so she grabbed her coat and bag and followed him a few moments later.

An elderly couple in matching raincoats and rain hats were in reception, and several customers were queuing behind them. Natalia caught a snatch of their conversation.

'Oh, I don't know, do you, Harold? The green line, I think. Yes, the green one ... it'll melt if we don't get it in the freezer soon.'

It was dark outside. Car and taxi head-lights flashed as they roared past. Here and there, Christmas lights twinkled in shop-window displays. Natalia looked down Baker

Street, then up. Cliff was sheltering in a shop doorway, lighting a cigarette. He'd told Stefan he had something for her. Had he *really* found Helen's missing items, or was that just a subterfuge to meet her? He was acting outside his normal curmudgeonly zone. And once she accepted his help, would he then feel he had a hold over her, a favour to call in?

But whichever it was, Helen Bookman took priority. She had to find out if Cliff had her belongings. She swallowed her doubts and approached.

'Hello, Cliff. Stefan says you have something for me?'

'Aye.' His eyes glittered in the darkness as he stared at her, then took a deliberate drag on his cigarette. 'It's under ma jacket.'

For a moment she thought he was going to demand something from her. Did he want money? But then he said, 'Here y'are lassie.' He opened his fleece jacket and passed her a handbag. She caught a whiff of tobacco smoke from his clothes, and she was transported back to Great Uncle Jan for a moment.

'Helen Bookman's handbag! You found it.'

'I thought mebbe you'd want me to keep quiet about finding it, seeing as someone decided to misplace it yesterday.'

Or you would rather no one knew items were going walkabout on your watch? she thought. 'Where was it hiding?'

'Well, erm, it was in the, erm, Special Items room.'

'Ah – that was the forbidden room I saw yesterday.'

'That's the one. Off-limits, that one is,' he said briskly. 'How the handbag got in there, I don't know.'

'Who has keys to this room?' She turned the bag over and inspected it. It was made from beautifully soft, expensive leather, bearing the distinctive Mulberry logo. She had an immediate vision of Avon coveting the bag, as she had the Jimmy Choos. Cliff must have read her mind. 'Senior management, of course, and me and Avon.'

She nodded. 'What about the shoes?'

'No sign yet. Well, you've got what you wanted.' He took a deep drag on his cigarette. 'What happens now?'

'I call Mr Bookman. He was here this morning.'

'Aye, I heard.' He watched Natalia intently. 'I'll be getting back now.'

'How was your meeting last night?' she asked.

'Meeting? What ... oh, that. It was fine.' He dropped his cigarette butt and ground it out with his heel, before shambling off.

Natalia looked at the bag again. It was quite big, but it had been very easy for Cliff to walk out with it without anyone noticing, despite Avon's security measures. She watched Cliff's departing back, and wondered to herself: *Could Cliff himself be the Hoaxer?* He seemed so straightforward and genuine at times, but could she trust him?

As she walked back towards the LPO entrance, she couldn't resist releasing the studded gold clasp of the bag and glancing inside. It felt like an illicit invasion of privacy, but she was drawn to the contents in an effort to understand Helen better. She wouldn't pry too deeply.

There was still a faint aroma of leather. A quick look revealed keys, a handkerchief, a compact mirror and lipstick, and credit cards. Her purse and mobile phone were not there. She must ask Peter Bookman if the police had checked her phone records to see if she had used it since Friday. And who she'd called that day. Surely they would have that information by now. Had Helen taken her mobile phone and purse with her, or had they been stolen before the bag was found and handed in?

She placed the Mulberry handbag over her shoulder as she crossed the office, and tried to look natural. If she was caught with the bag now, it could mean trouble for both herself and Cliff. Her mind was whirling – there was so much to think about. She knew her first priority should be to phone Peter Bookman, yet she found herself holding back. What would he say when she told him they had the bag but not the shoes? Surely he could not get upset about that. What was troubling her more was how she was going to tell him that his wife had left her possessions behind on purpose. How would he take that in? And should she call him or the police?

Once back at her desk, Natalia opened the deep file drawer, dropped the handbag in, then closed and locked it. She was popping the key inside her purse, when a shadow loomed over the desk. Her heart missed a beat. 'Oh!'

'Natalia.' Avon was standing in front of her, hands on her broad hips. 'What have you found out?'

'Found out?' Natalia was confused.

'In the CCTV room, about the Hoaxer.'

'Oh, nothing at all. I'm sorry.'

'Nothing?' Avon frowned, eyes narrowing behind her glasses. 'You're not holding back on me, are you? What's that Omar been saying?'

'It's very slow work. To be thorough, I've only looked at the past few days. I have not seen anything suspicious. Tomorrow, I go back over the past week.'

'What about the CCTV from our reception area?'

'All of us, going to and fro. Our customers, of course. The early-morning van bringing the lost items from stations and depots.'

Avon continued to frown. Finally she said, 'I have noticed these hoaxes started not long after you arrived. Don't think I haven't.' Then she walked off, leaving Natalia open-mouthed at her veiled accusation.

But she put her anger aside. The search for Helen came first. She turned to Sherlock again, to check the logging in details once more. This time she wanted to see whether Avon had double-checked the contents of the bag. She glanced up to see if anyone was watching. Stefan and Mark had their heads together – probably arguing over midfield positions, or central-defensive partnerships – while inside her office, Donna was bent over her desk.

She returned to the familiar details of the 'related items'. There was an asterisk beside the handbag and, yes, Avon had detailed the contents in a further file: keys, hand-kerchief, lipstick, a diary, a compact mirror – a *diary!*

Quickly she unlocked her drawer and looked inside the bag again.

The diary was no longer there.

10

Helen had had her diary with her when she left home that Friday morning. And that diary was still in the handbag when it had reached the Lost Property Office. Now it was missing. Where could it be?

She looked across at where Avon's magenta hair quivered as the woman fussed about her desk. She picked up the bag and marched over. This time it was *her* shadow that loomed over Avon.

'Remember this?' she asked, placing it on Avon's desk.

'What do you mean by–' the woman began to bluster, but the sight of the expensive handbag stopped her in her tracks. 'Oh, yes, I remember this one. What are *you* doing with it?'

'It belongs to the missing woman, Helen Bookman.'

'What missing woman?'

'The poster on the noticeboard. Over there.'

'Oh that. How do you know it's hers?'

'From CCTV footage, and from Sherlock's records. You logged it in. And you listed the contents. There was a diary in it.

And now the diary has gone.'

Avon chewed her lip, her skin turning even paler. 'Well, I haven't got it,' her bluster returned, and then she halted mid-flow. 'Wait a minute. The diary. It has to be! I thought I recognised it. My hoax, yesterday. The diary in the photograph, that was the diary from this bag. You have your answer. The Hoaxer has the diary.' Dismissing Natalia, she began to put on her coat.

'Wait a moment,' Natalia said. 'You can help, Avon. Tell me everything you remember about the diary.'

Avon tutted, but allowed Natalia to detain her. 'I remember it very well. It was very classy, just like the handbag. It was a Smythson diary. Shop in Regent Street, or is it Bond Street? Stationers to the royal family. It was a sort of peachy colour. There were initials embossed in the corner.' Her irritation faded and her face became dreamy.

'Were the initials HB?'

Avon's expression suddenly sharpened. Annoyed at being pulled out of her dream, she snapped, 'And what if they were? You say it belongs to the missing woman? You want to hand the case over to the police. Better still, Donna ought to call them. I could call her mobile.'

'No! No – there's no need to do that. I'm going to phone Mr Bookman.'

Avon peered at her suspiciously, her eyes

enlarged by the glasses she wore. 'What's in this for you then? Is there a reward?'

'No reward. But I think it's right Mr Bookman should take it to the police. They are looking for Helen, his wife, at his insistence.'

'I don't know.' Avon was reluctant to leave it to Natalia. 'I'm sure Donna would want us to call in the Met. She always does that when there's a hoax, and the diary was involved in a hoax. Anyway, you're as bad as Mark Thomas with all this time wasting. You're supposed to be finding the Hoaxer. That's your brief.'

'Believe me, I really want to find them.'

A faint hint of aftershave reached their nostrils. Stefan was heading towards them, looking especially attractive. Natalia could almost feel the magnetism of his physical presence drawing Avon away from her side. With relief, she felt Avon's attention shift away from her and the bag.

'Good night,' he said, blowing them a kiss. 'I wish I could take you with me, but I can't disappoint the girls at the nightclub. I'm the only thing they have to look forward to all day.' He winked and set off towards reception and the exit. But he'd done enough to distract Avon. She followed Stefan, trying to capture his attention, and disappeared into reception, as if completely forgetting that she'd been urging Natalia to phone the police about the handbag.

Natalia glanced at her watch. It was just six o'clock. Time enough to take another quick check at the records Avon had made on Sherlock of Helen's belongings. Could she have recorded any other details that Natalia hadn't noticed last night? Could anything else be missing?

As she worked, she suddenly remembered being shown an old-fashioned box file of dockets when she'd first started working at the LPO. She knew the box files were kept in Donna's office. The dockets were forms filled out at the point the lost objects were handed in. They were then passed along the line until the objects finally arrived in Baker Street.

It would make sense to double-check these dockets, just in case, but she'd have to wait until Avon had gone. And Avon, having failed to keep Stefan from leaving, seemed to be finding plenty to do at her desk. Doggedly, Natalia went through a cross-referencing search and made notes until at last, without saying goodbye, Avon put on her coat, wound a woolly scarf round her neck, pulled a little hat on her head, and left.

Natalia waited a beat, then went over to Donna's office and tried the door. It was open! No doubt so that Avon could use it, if she needed to. She was glad she would not have to ask Rasheda for the key and expose her to risk. She looked around at the empty office. No sign of Cliff, who would understand why she was doing this, nor were there sounds of the cleaners yet.

Feeling light headed, telling herself firmly not to feel guilty, she entered Donna's office and switched on the light. The big bird-of-paradise plant seemed to be watching her every move as she crossed to the box files, neatly arranged across the top of the free-standing cupboard. Above them, hanging on the wall, was a framed picture she'd not noticed yesterday when they'd all crammed in to see the hoaxes. It was of a man in sand-coloured combat fatigues, beret on his head, receiving a spear from a Zulu warrior. 'Colonel Harris being honoured' was the caption. Donna's father, she assumed.

Quickly, she picked out the relevant box file, laid it on top of the cupboard, opened it and began riffling through the contents. They were in date order, which made her task much easier. 'Found, Circle Line westbound silk scarf orange/yellow,' she read. 'Found Circle Line westbound, handbag, light-brown leather, clasp, contents: purse, wallet, keys, handkerchief, compact mirror, lipstick, diary.' Avon had remembered correctly. 'Found, Circle Line westbound, pair of high heels, brown. All items found together, handed in High Street Kensington station.'

She read through the bag's contents again. Everything apart from the diary was still in

112

the handbag. Lost in thought, Natalia stared at the pages, reviewing all the facts she'd discovered so far, including now the hoaxes and the Hoaxer. Did they use the Special Items room to store the objects they stole before use? Most importantly, what did they do with them afterwards? They had to be hidden somewhere. But no, it couldn't be the Special Items room, because Cliff would have spotted those Impala horns immediately. Unless... She prayed that the Hoaxer didn't take the articles away from the Lost Property Office, otherwise the diary would be beyond her reach.

'Looking for something?'

Natalia spun around then breathed a sigh of relief. Rasheda was grinning at her. Today her hair was tied up with a bright-yellow scarf and she wore a matching top.

'And found it,' she replied. 'How're you?'

'Nothing a week's sleep wouldn't cure. Those two boys of mine take a lot of running after. How are Connor and Nuala?' Rasheda asked as they left Donna's office.

'Connor's great. His mother took him to the dentist this morning. As for Nuala – teenage girls. Must be worse than boys.'

'You're not wrong there!' Rasheda said. 'But what are you doing working late up here? I thought you were sent to the basement to look at CCTV tapes.'

'I was. It's hard work to keep your concentration, but I managed it. And I saw the weirdest thing. Helen Bookman, the missing woman I was telling you about? First of all, I found that some of her belongings had been sent here. And then I saw her on CCTV. She didn't drop them. She put them on the train seat, then walked away. Shoes, scarf, handbag. She had some trainers to change into.'

'Strange indeed. You mean like she wanted people to find her things and think – what?'

'And why hasn't she at least contacted her mother or her closest friends? And now I've just learned that the office hoaxer has stolen Helen's diary – it was yesterday's hoax on Avon. Oh, and her shoes are missing.'

'Two steps forward, one back,' Rasheda sympathised. 'Do you think the Hoaxer knew the diary belonged to the missing woman?'

'I hope not. That would be scary. I don't think it would be a good idea to make an announcement about the diary. That might drive the Hoaxer into hiding, or make him destroy the diary if he still has it. You can see, I *must* work out who it is.'

'As long as you take care,' Rasheda advised.

'Yesterday I spent half an hour in the vault alone with Cliff after you'd gone.'

'Brrr,' Rasheda shuddered. 'You crazy girl.'

'He was helpful.'

'Maybe, but what's he after?'

'Not sure yet. I'd better let you get on and ring Dermot to say I'm on my way.'

'OK. You've got a good man there. See you.' The two women hugged briefly.

As she pulled on her coat, Natalia speed dialled Dermot.

'Oh, it's you,' he said, without his usual warmth. 'Where are you now?'

'What's wrong?'

'You mean, what's right?'

'What's happened!'

'Just tell me you're on your way, that's all I need to hear.'

'I'm leaving right this minute.'

'Thank goodness. Nuala and Connor are starving here. We'll have to go ahead and eat without you. Is that OK?'

'Nuala and ... oh my goodness, I'm so sorry. I'll be as quick as I can.'

'As long as you take care now.'

How could she have forgotten they were coming over tonight? Although, to be fair, they didn't usually see the kids this many times in a week. Their mother could be quite difficult on occasion, so when she'd suggested a few extra sleepovers that week, Dermot had jumped at the chance to spend more quality time with his kids. Although this week it looked like it was turning into more quantity than quality.

11

'Wow, so you could see a terrorist, or some-body, stealing something. Stuff like that?' Connor asked, shuffling the remains of a plateful of biscuits into his mouth.

Natalia had been describing her day in the CCTV room to him. He was sitting at the table with her, his handheld computer game put aside as he listened. He was wearing his favourite football shirt over jeans. Natalia had been talking between bites of her pizza and salad. Dermot and Nuala sat, not speaking, at either end of the sofa. Nuala had a whole tub of Ben & Jerry's ice cream, which she was spooning slowly into her mouth while staring at the television. Natalia could tell from the tension in Dermot's neck and shoulders that he was upset with his daughter. Some time this evening they'd fallen out, but as yet she did not know why. She felt an overpowering wave of affection for her husband, but she held back from touching him. She sensed that the kids were not comfortable yet with overt signs of affection between them.

'I didn't see anybody breaking the laws today,' she said, 'except for a few fare dodgers. But I did see something very strange.' She hesitated. Should she mention Helen? Maybe, as long as she didn't give her name, or the full details. She had Connor's rapt attention.

'You know, at the Lost Property Office we look after things that people forget and leave behind – books, bags, umbrellas, even laptops. That's when people are absent minded. But today, I saw a woman who put her scarf, handbag and shoes down beside her, then got off the train, on purpose.'

'Were they old things she didn't want?'

'No, they were expensive, new and special things.'

'Mmm.' Connor played with his game for a bit while Natalia finished her salad, then he said, 'Like she was laying a trail. Or planting clues! Or maybe she wants to give everything away and go and live on the streets. People do, you know?' he said sagely.

Natalia nodded. She wondered which of those had motivated Helen, if any. Perhaps the police were right and she didn't want to be found, intending to start a new life elsewhere. In which case, what had happened to make her behave so irrationally? Why hadn't she talked to her husband or mother? If she had met someone else, surely she'd have told a friend about him – or could it be a her, and she wasn't ready to come out yet? She came to with a start and noticed Connor was staring at her. This was no good. She must stop thinking about Helen Bookman. She'd already allowed her to intrude too much on family life today.

'Anyone want a drink?' she asked.

'I'll have a beer,' Dermot said.

'Coke!' Connor shouted.

Nuala, predictably, ignored Natalia's question.

When she'd given Dermot his beer, she said to Connor as she gave him his Coke, 'Mark, one of the young men in our office, plays fantasy football. He was told off for playing it all the time. How's your league coming on, Connor?'

'Team, not league!' he said, but proceeded to tell her about it in detail.

Afterwards, Natalia went into the kitchen to tidy away. When she slid the crusts of her pizza into the bin, she saw nearly a whole pizza in there. Nuala, she thought, with a flare of exasperation. She could just picture the scene. Dermot, wanting to please, still being made to feel obscurely guilty for the break-up of his marriage five years ago, would have caved in to Nuala and Connor's demands, buying the most expensive pizzas with bizarre toppings. Then Nuala would have taken only one bite of hers. Dermot would have remonstrated with her, and she would have stomped off in a sulk taking the ice cream with her for consolation.

Her heart went out to her husband. No wonder he'd sounded upset that she'd be late home from work. Nuala played up less when she was around. Maybe because she wanted to appear grown-up. But with her daddy, she could play the little girl. Dermot struggled to find the right way to cope, but those few years apart had created a gap they were both still trying to close – for Connor, life was simple. He had his daddy back, and that was enough for him. But there was still some anger in Dermot, and it was as if Nuala sensed it and was trying to make him explode. It was an emotional tightrope, she thought.

Standing there, she was nearly knocked flying by Nuala, who stormed past her with a face like thunder, rushing into the bathroom and slamming the door. Natalia heard the sound of the door being locked as Dermot appeared.

'That girl – what is it now?' he asked, not really expecting an answer.

'What happened?'

'I don't know. I just asked, to be civil like, how was school today, when she snapped my head off for being nosy and interfering, and what did I know about anything anyway? Then off she went. Maybe you can get some sense out of her.'

'I'll try.' They clasped hands for a moment, then Natalia went to the bathroom door and knocked.

'Nuala? Are you all right? Can I get you anything?'

'Oh, for heaven's sake. I just – want – to – be – left – alone!' Nuala yelled.

'Well, don't spend too long in there. Someone'll be wanting to use the loo, I expect. Why not go into your bedroom?'

'Go – away!' There was the sound of rattling and slamming as Nuala vented her anger on various objects in the bathroom.

'OK, I'll go for now. But we'd like to help. When you decide to come out.' Natalia listened for a bit longer. Could she hear the sound of sobs? For the first time, she began to feel really concerned about Nuala. This wasn't the usual teenage tantrums. Something more serious was going on.

'Time to get off the back seat, Natalia,' she told herself. 'Not today, but some time soon I'm going to get to the bottom of this. For all our sakes.'

Later, Natalia sat in front of the bedroom mirror, removing her make-up. She saw Dermot's reflection as he came in and collapsed onto the bed, sighing with exhaustion.

'How is she?'

'The little madam is behaving now as if noihing happened.' They'd decided to leave Nuala alone in the bathroom and, after half an hour, they'd heard her come out and go to her room. Once Connor was tucked up,

Natalia and Dermot decided to go to bed, too, and he'd just popped his head round Nuala's door. 'She's sitting up, in her pyjamas, reading a book, looking as if she'd never throw a tantrum in her life.'

'I'll just say good night, too, then.' Natalia stood up, but Dermot caught her wrist.

'Before you do, there's something I want to say.'

She sat down again on the stool, and he sat upon the edge of the bed, facing her with a serious expression.

'I understand that you'd like to help find this missing woman, Helen Bookman, but I'm concerned. Searching for her seems to be taking over your life. And why did you bring her handbag home with you?"

'I didn't want to risk leaving it just in case the Hoaxer took it. I know, I know, I could've locked it in my drawer. I don't know.' She waved her hands helplessly.

'All right, that was speculation; this is fact. Peter Bookman is not emotionally stable right now, and that's understandable. The man sounds like he's a pressure cooker about to blow. I think this is one instance where you should back off and leave it to the professionals.'

'Even if those professionals seem to have put his case as low priority?'

'Says who? Says Peter Bookman. You only have his angle on the whole thing. For all we know, the police really are out there looking for her.'

'But that doesn't make Helen's plight any less important, does it? Besides, you said yourself this is something I am good at. I know I can help.'

'No one's doubting your ability or your motives.' His voice softened. 'But I don't want you getting caught up in a situation where you might be, not to put too fine a point on it, threatened. Know what I mean?'

'I don't believe I am in any danger.'

'What about him coming down and shouting at you in the office? Good thing Stefan was there to see him off. And now he's had even less sleep, and even more stress and fear.' He took her hands in his. His navy-blue eyes took on a grey look when he was being serious. 'I know how much it means to you, making connections, reuniting people. I just don't want anything to happen to you, my love. I don't want to lose you.'

Moved, Natalia blinked away a tear. 'I will arrange to take the handbag to him in his office. There will be people all round us. I promise to be careful. All right?'

'All right. I don't mean to be telling you where you can go or who you can talk to. I just want you to think about what I've said. Leave it to the police.'

'OK. But if I find the diary—'

'It's your decision, but I'd like you to take

it to the police.' He leaned forward and kissed her on the lips. 'OK? Now hurry up and come to bed.'

12

As the nifty Docklands Light Railway train sped her towards Canary Wharf the following afternoon, Natalia gazed across the curious landscape of East London, with its mix of graceful ancient churches with steeples, and standardised warehousing punctuated by dirty-brick, Victorian pubs and modern houses. There was also much derelict ground where shrubs and wildflowers struggled gamely for survival. But she was only half aware of the landscape. In the canvas bag on the floor was Helen's expensive Mulberry handbag. Would Peter Bookman be aware Helen's diary was missing? Did he know she'd had it in her bag with her when she left their home?

In her own handbag was a copy of the CCTV tape showing Helen's last actions before she disappeared nearly a week ago.

When she'd phoned Peter this morning to arrange a time to deliver them, he had sounded so desolate that her heart had gone out to him again. Then, when he'd heard her news, that feverish hope returned again to his voice. When he viewed the tape, though, surely his torment would be excruciating. She hoped he would watch it after she'd gone. She didn't want to be at the brunt of his anger again. But at the same time, she was curious to see his reaction for herself.

She'd asked Omar if she could leave early, explaining that she wanted to take Helen's bag to Peter, and he'd agreed with that characteristic flick of his hand, aloof as ever. But she was grateful for his indifference. If she'd had to ask Avon, she'd have faced an interrogation and probable 'no'.

The train slowed, high upon its elevated rails, as it approached Canary Wharf. She had been catching glimpses of the River Thames, its water sparkling pink from the red-and-pink frosty winter sunset. They had passed the squat, silver-grey shape of the Dome at Bermondsey. Ahead now lay the soaring black glass and steel obelisk of Canary Wharf Tower, where Peter Bookman worked. The area around its base was a maze of small water lakes, edged with leafless trees and small bushes.

Walkways led her effortlessly into the lobby of the building, where she reported in, to find that Peter Bookman had left a message with the security men in reception that she was coming. Once she'd filled in the security book, and been given a pass, she headed for the lifts. She passed smartly dressed men and woman, heading out of the building, along with two bike messengers, helmets removed. The lift she got into was empty. All the same, she felt conscious of all the security cameras watching her ascent beyond the fifteenth floor.

As the doors opened, she saw Peter Bookman. Security must have alerted him and he'd come to meet her. 'Mrs O'Shea,' he said, oddly formal. 'Come with me.' And then he rushed her along a mottled grey-and-black marble corridor, punched in a security code and led her through a mahogany door. She had a quick glimpse of a reception desk, an open-plan office, a handful of people, and then they were in his office. It was a large corner office with breathtaking views. Natalia's head swam, as her vertigo kicked in. She concentrated on looking at the shiny desk, the low chairs for meetings, the green plants, and cabinets. Framed artwork of bold abstracts with vibrant colours hung on the walls. But Natalia was most drawn to an artistic black-and-white portrait of Helen.

'Coffee?' he asked. There was a Cona machine, the jug half full.

'Thank you, just with milk please.'

She went up to the photo and studied it. The photographer had captured just head and bared shoulders. Round her neck was a chunky piece of metal jewellery and her head was tilted slightly, an enigmatic smile on her face. Peter came to stand behind her. 'Good, isn't it. I commissioned it just after we were married, ten years ago, but Helen hasn't changed a bit. She's just as beautiful.' He handed her a cup of coffee, then took a sip of his own. Looking at Helen's photo seemed to calm him. 'And these paintings are by Helen. She's very talented. Though she works in finance like I do – that's how we met – in her spare time she paints and sometimes helps out in a painting class at the local community centre with local kids, too.

'It's something we've talked about. I said I'd support her if she wanted to, but she said not yet. Because ... well, because.' He waved her towards the low chairs.

Natalia sat down on one of the low visitor chairs and carefully put down her cup, then got out Helen's handbag and placed it on the coffee table. Peter placed his own cup on the glass coffee table, put his mobile phone beside him, then rubbed his hands together, as if they were sweaty. She saw the dark circles around his eyes. His hands were visibly trembling and his clothes looked crumpled, as if he hadn't changed for days. Slept in them? Unlikely, probably paced and dozed all night, waiting for the phone to ring.

'I can't tell you,' he said, his voice breaking up, 'how grateful I am for your help.'

'I'm glad to do it.'

126

He reached out and touched Helen's bag and it seemed to calm him. 'You didn't bring her shoes?'

'We're still looking for them.'

'No shoes? Well, they're not important.' He appeared to be unconcerned. She was relieved that he didn't question her further about where the bag had been. She'd told him it had been misplaced, nothing more.

'Any news from the police?' she asked. 'Has Helen called? Have they been able to trace her mobile phone calls?'

He shook his head. 'They say they are following the usual lines of enquiry – whatever those are. And she's not used her mobile since last Thursday. There were no unusual numbers called, either, they were all people I know. At least she's been gone long enough for them to register her as officially missing.' He suddenly looked up directly at her, revealing the wretchedness deep in his eyes. She found his naked gaze disconcerting.

'But what was it you said? About seeing Helen on CCTV? Something strange – damn!' he said as his mobile rang. He snatched it up, the flash of expectancy in his eyes painful to see. When he heard the voice at the other end, he almost grimaced. 'No, nothing from the police,' he said impatiently. 'Yes?' He listened for a moment, then said, 'Yes, I'm sure she had enough tablets on her. Wait a minute.' He opened Helen's handbag and looked through it. 'She must have them with her. There's none in the bag – yes, the Lost Property Office have just brought it – and there were none left at home.' He listened again, then said shortly, 'Yes, yes, of course I'll phone as soon as there's news – anything.' He dropped the phone beside him on the chair. 'Helen's mother,' he explained. 'She phones me twice a day. What can I tell her? I wish I could reassure her that I am trying. I don't see what more I could do.' He bowed his head in despair and ran his hands through his dark hair. She saw, that it was beginning to thin a little on the crown.

'The tablets,' Natalia asked. When she'd heard him mention tablets she had begun to feel alarmed. 'Is Helen a diabetic? Does she have a heart condition? What are they for?'

He looked up. 'No, nothing like that. She doesn't have a serious medical condition.'

'They must be for something,' Natalia persisted. 'If her mother thinks they're important.'

'Well, Helen had been feeling a bit – a bit low recently. So the doctor prescribed some tablets. A sort of mild antidepressant.'

'Would they be worth money on the streets? Could someone have stolen them before the handbag was handed in?'

Peter shook his head. 'I shouldn't think so. They had some long name, and they're not very strong. Thing is, Helen's mother has always worried about her too much. She's her only child.'

'She loves her daughter.'

'Maybe so, but she should have more faith in her. She says she's too sensitive and will fall apart without her tablets.'

'And would she?'

'I don't think so.'

'Did she – did she have a lot of them, do you know?' Natalia's mind went off on another tack.

'No, no. I already checked with her doctor – the police asked me to. She's got about a week's worth, and it takes several days after that before the effect wears off. That wouldn't make her behave irrationally.'

Natalia pictured the woman she'd seen, with that frozen, shocked look on her face, deliberately leaving her handbag, her scarf. Deliberately removing her shoes. Had she seemed about to go on a voyage of self harming? Were her actions premeditated or spur of the moment? It had been impossible to tell. She could have been carrying a second pair of shoes for some other reason.

'Peter, we'll have to fill in some paperwork to verify the handbag as Helen's. Is there anything in it that might give a clue as to where she was going last Friday?'

He picked it up and looked through it again, this time more slowly, examining each item minutely, even opening the lipstick.

'Nothing,' he sighed. 'All quite normal.' He did not mention her diary. 'The CCTV of Helen, you were going to–'

Natalia opened her mouth to give Peter a more detailed account of what she'd seen of Helen on the CCTV, when there was a knock on his door.

'Not again! Come in,' he barked, and an attractive woman entered. Her copper-coloured hair was cut short in a stylish bob, and she had large, topaz-coloured eyes. Her gaze rested on Natalia with curiosity.

'Miss Parsons. I'm in a meeting.' Peter's voice was curt.

'Oh, I'm sorry, I didn't realise you had someone with you,' she said, but made no move to leave and there was an awkward silence. 'It was just, I couldn't help over-hearing that you were talking about Helen. Is there any news of her?'

'This is Natalia O'Shea, from the Lost Property Office,' Peter introduced her coolly. 'Tanya Parsons, one of my colleagues.'

Tanya shook Natalia's hand. Her fingers and palm were so slender they felt like a child's. Immediately she turned back to Peter.

'Has Helen been found?' she asked. 'I've been thinking about her.' She turned back to Natalia, a slight smile touching her glossed lips. 'Helen is always so well organised – coming into the office, doing her painting, even voluntary work. This seems so ... out of character.'

'It's very worrying,' Natalia agreed.

'All the office are behind you, Peter. We're here for you, whatever may happen,' Tanya said softly and reached out to touch his arm only for him to flinch and pull away, almost cuffing her in the process. Natalia was stunned by the physicality of his response, as was the woman who hurriedly dropped her hand, saying, 'I'll leave you to it then', not before giving Natalia another curious look before ducking out.

When the door closed behind her he said, almost to himself, 'If one more person asks me for news, when there isn't any, I swear I'll–' He hunched over and rubbed his hands across his face, then he looked up. 'Tell me about the CCTV.'

For some inexplicable reason, the mood in Peter's office had changed. As if talking about his wife with a colleague had un-settled him. Once again, Natalia began to feel uneasy in the company of this man. She realised that she had built a picture of him based on his torment. But what did she really know about him? He'd just been incredibly hostile to a work colleague who'd only been expressing concern. He'd barely been civil to Helen's mother, too. There was no warmth in his tones for his mother-in-law, who must be feeling just as bad as he was, longing for news of her beloved only daughter. Perhaps this crisis had stripped away his veneer and this was his real attitude to women. If so, what did this new revelation mean for Helen?

Natalia took a sip of her bitter coffee. It was all bringing up unwanted memories. She told herself to stay calm, and to leave as soon as she could.

She began to describe what she had seen. 'It looked to me as if your wife knew exactly what she was doing.'

Peter raised his head and stared at her aghast, then he jumped up and began striding about the office in agitation. 'I can't believe it. Why would she do that? It can't be true!' He turned and stood over her, his face twisted with conflicting emotions. 'When I left for work, she was just the same as usual. She even–' he gave a cold laugh. 'She even asked me what I wanted for supper. How can she do this to me? Doesn't she know how she's torturing me?'

Natalia stared up at him, her heart racing. His fists were clenched, his jaw working. Everything he said was about himself. Did he have any thought for Helen's feelings?

'What happened next, Peter, after she asked you about supper?' She hoped she kept her voice from wavering, as she reached out to calm him with the cool touch of her hand.

He stared down at her hand and for a moment Natalia wondered whether he was going to flick her off, too. Was he even contemplating hitting her? But she met his gaze evenly. Then he recollected himself and slumped back on the chair opposite and continued his story of last Friday morning.

'Helen was having a flexi-time day, working at home. Normally we travel to work here together – she's a couple of floors below with the accounts team – anyway, I said I didn't mind, something from the freezer would do. What a stupid thing to say. Why didn't I tell her I loved her? That I wanted to take her out. What an idiot.' He suddenly stopped. 'I suppose the police are going to have a field day.'

Very much wanting to leave now, Natalia stood up. 'I made a copy of the tape,' she took a memory stick from her bag and handed it to him. 'For the police.'

'Of course, of course.' He tried to sound more in control. 'I'm sorry, for all this.' He waved his arms. 'I'm not normally like this. Give me the money markets and I can handle anything, but this ... I don't know how to cope. You will stay in touch, won't you?' he pleaded.

'I will,' she promised, reminding herself she was keeping an open mind. She paused by the door. 'What did you mean, *the police will have a field day?*'

'They made it perfectly clear. They think she's bolted – left me.'

'Why would they think that?'

Peter shrugged. He seemed to collapse, shrink away. The storm had passed and he was now the man she had first met. 'I don't know. They keep saying that's the most likely reason. A domestic of some kind. But we haven't had any more arguments than most. Every marriage has its ups and downs and I'm not denying we're any different. But I'm sure she hasn't met someone else. I'd just know.'

It seemed the lift took forever to arrive, and then stopped at every floor, but at last Natalia could escape the building. Outside in the dark, Natalia took deep breaths of fresh air. Her body felt as if she'd been physically battered and she realised just how tensely she'd been holding herself. Without thinking, she began walking on the wooden boarding around the water, staring down into its smooth, reflective surface.

She remembered in minute detail the last time she'd felt like this. It was exactly four years ago. She'd been standing over the sink in the kitchen, scrubbing brush in hand and suds rising, when suddenly the man she loved, the man she'd called husband, erupted. Jem's voice had turned thick and ugly with fury and hatred. The veins stood out in his neck and his handsome face was

134

distorted with rage. Abuse poured from his mouth, in English and Turkish and Polish. He said terrible things, things about her which were untrue but she'd be ashamed for anyone else to ever hear.

She'd feared he would strike her. His hand was raised on several occasions, as he pounded the small ceramic tiles on their kitchen wall and, at one point, kicked a hole through the kitchen door. Somehow she'd found the right survival mechanism. She pretended quiet dignity, she didn't argue back, she didn't reply, but she didn't cower.

Later he apologised, he was as loving as always. She even tended his foot, pulling off his boot, cradling it in the bathroom. He was sorry – the pressures on him were so extreme, he didn't know what to do, he'd simply exploded. He loved her so much, she was his world, his everything. He couldn't live without her. They would talk it all through, there had to be a compromise they could reach.

But it didn't happen. Instead, that became the first of several times over the next few months. The darkest period of her life. She would lie silently in bed beside him, eyes wide open in the dark, waiting for him to fall asleep. Only then would she feel safe enough to sleep herself. Until, one night, he woke her by leaning over her and hissing in her ear, that she was no good, an unfit mother – she tuned out his words. Eventually he fell back to sleep, but she lay awake the rest of the night. She would push back the covers and pad through to the small box room next door, standing over the small bed where Paul, their son, slept soundly, grateful that he had not heard his father.

The morning after, it was as if nothing had happened. He kissed her goodbye, hugged Paul. But Natalia knew she could not spend a single night longer under the same roof. She packed a bag for her and one for Paul, phoned her work and said she was ill, then got in her little car and drove to her parents' house. She left everything. The home they'd lovingly created – she wanted none of it, tainted by his unreasoning anger.

A tiny flame deep inside her knew that the woman he heaped abuse on was not really her – it sprang out of his own psyche, created by the terrible pressures of society and family and who knew what else in his nature. A fault line then developed and the dark stuff spewed out, like lava from a volcano. And then what had followed became the greatest betrayal of all, bringing in its wake a never-ending heartache. She raised her hands to her hot cheeks and brushed away the tears.

Peter Bookman had brought this all back. Was that what he had been like with Helen? Was that his true nature? In which case,

Natalia understood only too well why she had left. Perhaps even now she was starting a new life for herself, a life without fear. As Natalia had done.

Was her intention to help actually no better than meddling, and was it the worst thing to do, to reunite Helen with Peter? It seemed now that Dermot's advice was right. Rasheda was so right, too. She had a good man there. During the growth of their love, as she and her family helped Dermot come to terms with his divorce and to calling his children again, so something that was broken within her had healed, too.

She took a deep breath. She'd probably overreacted. It still happened occasionally. Nothing had changed. Helen needed to be found, if for her own sake now, thinking of her tablets, and not for Peter's.

Natalia's mobile rang. She groped in her handbag and answered it.

'Hello, you,' Dermot's voice sounded as if he was standing right beside her, his breath tickling her ear. 'What's cooking?'

'I'll tell you later.' The sound of his voice brought a wave of warmth to her. 'Everything all right?'

'Ah, not really. I'm sorry to do this, Nat, I really am but could you go to Nuala's school? They've just phoned and asked if someone can fetch her. Kathleen can't go, she's on the motorway coming down from

Cambridge. She was going to pick her up after rehearsals on her way home. Connor's staying over with a school friend. I'd go, but we're in the middle of something tricky and I can't really leave.'

Dermot had to be involved in something very important at the site not to be able to respond to the school's request, Natalia knew.

'Don't worry. I'll be there in about forty-five minutes.'

'Thanks, darlin'. I'll tell her teacher you're on your way.'

13

Natalia had to pass through two locked entrances at Nuala's school. First was the school gate. It was set in a high perimeter fence with sharp, curving points at the top. It was not designed so much to stop kids getting out, as to deter miscreants from climbing over and vandalising the school buildings at night and at the weekends. In the past autumn alone, one boy had tried to set fire to it, while a gang of boys and girls had thrown stones at the windows. She could see a few youths now, gathered outside the nearby newsagents' shop, but they were intent on business of their own and ignored her.

Having announced herself at the front gate, she then waited for the janitor to let her in the main door. Once inside the building, the familiar smells of schools met her. Despite the computer age, the use of whiteboards, the advent of café-style canteens, underneath you could still smell industrial floor polish, books and chalk.

'This set of stairs, first floor, turn left, door marked Room Eleven, Mrs O'Shea,' the janitor told her, then returned to his warm cubby hole.

At the bottom of the stairs she paused. She could hear the faint sounds of music and accompanying singing, it was a current top-ten hit. That would be the Christmas show rehearsals going on. Nuala would be very disappointed if she were missing them. It was the one thing she'd shown some enthusiasm for lately, and she'd been hoping to get a solo spot.

Natalia knocked on the door of Room Eleven and went in. She recognised Miss Ogwala from parents' evening. She was Nuala's form teacher and also took her for social studies. Her hair was sprinkled with grey and cut very close to her head, and she wore a neat skirt and jacket that hung on her bony frame. She was sitting at her desk, while the hunched form of Nuala, picking her nails rather than reading the book in front of her, sat at a front desk. She always looked smaller and younger in her school uniform, even if it always was a wreck by the end of the day. Natalia was relieved to see no sign of serious injury, no bandages or sticking plasters.

'Good evening, Miss Ogwala. Thank you for calling us. How are you, Nuala? Are you OK?'

'Nuala is in good health,' Miss Ogwala said. 'Which is more than I can say for the other girl.'

'Were there two involved? I'm sorry to hear that.'

'It generally takes two to have a fight,' Nuala's teacher observed dryly.

Natalia couldn't take, in what she was saying. 'A fight? Who attacked them?'

'No one attacked *them*, Mrs O'Shea. It was Nuala who was doing the attacking, and we have the full cast as witnesses.'

'Nuala attacking? There must be some reason. She must have been provoked in some way. I'd like to hear Nuala's side of the story.'

'You're welcome to try.'

They both looked at Nuala, but she scrunched defiantly further down into her seat and refused to look at them.

'Well, nothing like this has ever happened before. There has to be a–'

'Oh, but it has. We have had occasion to speak to Nuala several times in the past two months. Did you not get the letters?'

Looking at the girl, Natalia slowly shook her head. 'Nuala lives with her mother, and stays with her father and me a couple of nights a week. Her mother, Kathleen, hasn't mentioned any letters.'

'What I can tell you is that this is Nuala's final warning. We have decided to remove her from the Christmas show. For the safety of the other pupils you understand. We have zero tolerance of bullying in this school. It must be stamped out.'

'Bullying!' Natalia's mind refused to accept what the teacher was telling her. 'I still think there must be some mistake.'

'I can assure you that Nuala pushed the girl, pulled her hair and when she attempted to protect herself, Nuala knocked her to the ground.'

Was that a sly smile on the teenager's face?

'Both her father and yourself, and her mother, need to speak to Nuala about this. We can't allow any pupil to become a victim.'

'What happens now?'

'You must take Nuala home. She's no longer welcome at rehearsals, and we'll be having a meeting about her, then we can talk further. A sign of contrition or remorse would not go amiss.'

141

Miss Ogwala's clipped tones echoed in Natalia's head as she shepherded Nuala from the classroom. She was relieved that Nuala came with her without protest, though she did not speak once on the short journey home on the bus. Natalia welcomed the time to gradually absorb this shocking new picture of the girl. All this time Dermot and she had been worrying about her, had even discussed the possibility that Nuala might be the target of a bully or a gang. There were so many new forms of torture school kids could inflict on each other as they fought to establish their pecking order, using mobile phones and computers to spread the humiliation, pain and fear they visited on each other.

But it was Nuala who was making someone else's life a hell.

'Where's my dad?' was the only thing Nuala said as they entered the flat.

'He'll be home in an hour.' Natalia gave no further explanation. Anything she said might be used as fuel for anger by this troubled teenager.

Nuala flung herself on the sofa and plugged her iPod firmly into her ears. She began to hum, her eyes closed. So that was how it was going to be. Natalia made some sandwiches, some tea for herself, and carried them in. She placed some of the sandwiches and a glass of milk near Nuala, then sat at the table and opened her newspaper. An idea was beginning to form in her mind. She sat quietly for awhile, reading, while eating sandwiches and drinking her tea. Out of the corner of her eye, she saw Nuala eat a couple of sandwiches, and that she began increasingly to glance towards her.

Wait, she counselled herself. She remembered being on her uncle's farm once, when she was young. He'd been taming a wild colt. Her uncle had put treats in his pocket and stood without looking at the animal. Gradually it calmed down, then approached him. He spoke soothingly to it, looking down non-confrontationally, fed it treats, and gradually the agitation and resistance left the animal.

Nuala took the iPod from her ears. 'Is there some Coke? I hate milk.'

Natalia didn't look up, thinking, last week you loved milk! 'In the kitchen, help yourself,' she said.

While Nuala was out of the room, Natalia fetched a photograph album from the bookshelf. When the girl returned she said, 'Join me, Nuala, there's something I'd like to show you.'

Nuala groaned but sat beside her at the table, looking anything but interested.

'These are my family photographs. I haven't shown them to you before.' She began to turn the pages. 'This was my grandparents' wedding. See, they're in traditional costume. They were from the country.' She turned the pages quickly through her father growing upon the farm with his brothers and sisters, and then her own parents' wedding in the local Catholic church. 'Despite the Communist regime, Poland was able to keep the Church.'

While keeping her face turned away, Nuala was peering down at the photos, affecting boredom. Natalia began to tell some happy anecdotes from her own childhood. It was when she reached the move from country to city, and the big changes it brought that Nuala stiffened and burst out angrily, 'What do I care about your stupid brothers and sisters, your stupid family. Happy families. It's all crap. Bet you were all miserable anyway.' Then she burst into tears.

Natalia resisted the urge to hug her and comfort her. She had to learn to feel and then deal with her emotions. She let her cry for a bit then said, 'There are many different kinds of family. Your father and mother don't live together, but they both love you.'

'No, they don't!' Nuala shouted, then bowed her head to the table and gave way to more noisy sobs. Her shoulders shook. 'I hate everybody.'

Natalia was surprised that Nuala was accusing her mother as well as her father. She thought all the girl's rage was reserved for Dermot, and so did he.

'Your mum loves you,' she said firmly.

Nuala raised her head, face blotchy with tears. 'All she cares about is her stupid boy-friend – stupid Nathan. He's always round our house, or she's out with him and me and Connor have a horrible babysitter.'

'Your mother is entitled to meet someone new.' Connor had mentioned a Nathan, but they hadn't realised he was a serious new boyfriend of Kathleen's.

'But what about us, me and Connor? Supposing she wants to live with him. He's got three children already. Where will we go? There won't be room for us.' She choked on these last words then wept again, more qui-etly this time. Natalia waited for more of the pain to be released.

'That's something we would sit down and discuss. All of us. When it happens, or even *if* it happens. It might not happen at all. Your mother might go off this new man. Or he might go off her.'

Nuala swung her legs to and fro, sniffing and hiccupping. 'I didn't really mean it,' she said. 'I told her she was a silly, ugly cow. And she stank. Which is true.'

'Was that the other girl?'

Nuala nodded. 'I said she was a nerdy loser. Well, she is, no one likes her. People say those sorts of things all the time. Anyway, she said something to me I didn't

145

like so I ... you know.'

'And did you feel better? For saying those things?'

Nuala fidgeted uncomfortably. 'Maybe. No.'

'What's Nathan like?'

'I hate him. He tries to be all friendly. Connor likes him 'cos they play computer games together. He's just a kid.'

'How does he try to be friendly?'

Nuala was one step ahead of her and made a face. 'Not like that. Nothing like ... you know. He's just all smiley and jokey, like everything's all right but he doesn't mean it, he just wants *her*. Mum.'

'She likes him. She wants to be with him.'

'We don't go shopping together any more, she doesn't have time. Or watch TV like we used to, just the two of us when Connor is m bed. He's always there.'

'Nuala, listen to me. I don't have easy words for you. Sometimes life is tough, and then we have to deal with it. You are having to share your mother for the first time. You're hurting and you're jealous because she wants to spend time with someone other than you. But sometimes we have to put up with things we don't like. For the sake of someone else.' Nuala's jaw was beginning to set rebelliously, so Natalia hurried on. 'Remember this, you've had your mum to yourself for twelve years, especially in the past five years since she split up with your dad. You are her daughter. She will always have the same amount of love for you. She's not taking that away and giving it to Nathan instead. Gradually, things will settle down.'

'I s'pose.'

'There's no need to panic about the future. We can all talk about that. Perhaps we can have a family conference, and you can ask for some time each week for just you and your mum.'

Nuala went red. 'She won't listen. And then she'll hate me.'

'No, she won't. Maybe she thinks you're busy with your own life, but if you don't tell her she won't know. Sometimes when we're hurting we lash out, like you did today. But that's not the answer. Hurting other people is not the answer.'

'Mmm.' Nuala had got out her mobile phone and seemed to be more interested in it than what Natalia was saying. Then she said. 'It's Thursday night. Dad always goes out for a drink with his mates. He doesn't have to come back specially for me.'

'Why don't you give him a ring and talk about it? I'll go and see what's in the freezer for supper.'

14

'Come in, come in.' Rasheda enveloped Natalia in a hug.

'This is Dermot.' Natalia beamed, introducing her husband.

'Good to meet you.' Rasheda shook his hand, smiling broadly. Dermot leaned forward and gave her a kiss on the cheek. 'And we brought you a bottle or two.' He held up the bag he was carrying.

'Excellent! You said the magic words. Come on up. You'll see some familiar faces from work, Natalia, as well as my friends. I'm really glad you were able to come. I've made so much food, I'd've died if no one turned up to eat it!'

Rasheda had announced her impromptu party on Friday, for Saturday night. 'I want to have everyone round before they get all booked up for Christmas parties,' she'd told Natalia.

She led the way from the entrance hall, with its black-and-white tiled floor and wainscot panelling, set off above by dark, forest-green paint, upstairs to her first-floor flat. The stair carpet was a deep-brown, the banisters painted white.

'How long have you lived here?' Dermot asked.

'I moved in just before Danny was born, so the boys would have a room each: That's, oh my God, ten years ago! This old Victorian terrace was completely run down in those days, but we got a new freeholder who cared about the property, and now it's all done up.'

Rasheda was wearing a deep-red silk tunic over tight blue jeans, with a pair of red strappy sandals. Natalia felt a bit pale beside her in her ice-blue strapless dress, with a white angora shrug over the top. She'd managed to persuade her fine straight hair to go up tonight, and hoped it would stay in place. Dermot wore his smart jeans with a leather belt and an open-necked blue shirt under a jacket. 'I'm over forty now,' he'd said as they got ready. 'I wear my shirt inside my trousers.' His curly black hair had a sprinkling of iron grey, but Natalia's heart still turned over when she saw him unexpectedly.

Rasheda winked and made signs of approval behind his back as they went into her living room. Natalia glimpsed a Victorian fireplace with tiled surround and the room was painted in neutral colours.

'I'll get you a drink then introduce you to a few people. What'd you like?'

While Rasheda fetched white wine for Natalia and red for Dermot, they chatted to her downstairs neighbours about the pros and cons of living in Highbury versus Hackney. Then, glasses in hand, Natalia led Dermot over to say hello to Stefan. He was talking to a very attractive young woman in a skimpy black dress.

'Hi, there.' He kissed Natalia on both cheeks, then shook Dermot's hand. They'd met a couple of times before. 'This is Honey, Jason's girlfriend.' As he introduced her, she smiled then excused herself. Stefan sighed.

'She's off the market, Stefan,' Dermot said.

'I always like a challenge,' Stefan said. 'What has Jason got that I haven't?'

'A uniform?' Dermot joked and the two men clinked glasses.

'Avon is here,' Stefan told them. 'And Mark.'

'Not Cliff?'

'Aha, I want to meet Mr McDougall,' Dermot said, pretending to look severe. 'I think he has designs on my wife.'

Stefan nearly choked on his beer, and shook his head. 'Rasheda ask me to ask him, but he said, no. He is busy.'

Natalia raised her brows. 'He always seems busy in the evenings. What does he get up to, Stefan?'

'He talks about television sometimes. He likes sport. Basketball, boxing...'

'Does he belong to a gym?' Dermot asked.

Natalia and Stefan looked at each other.

'Difficult to tell how fit he is under those clothes he wears,' Natalia said.

'I tell him, please wear another colour jumper, but always grey or pale-brown,' Stefan said. 'I offer to take him shopping, he say, no.'

'He wears a big, shapeless jumper over baggy corduroy trousers,' Natalia explained. 'And thick-soled shoes.'

'He's always creeping up on me in them,' Stefan agreed.

Natalia felt a hand on her arm. It was Honey. 'I've brought Jason to meet you,' she said shyly.

'Haven't quite lost my touch then,' Stefan murmured in her ear.

'Behave!' Natalia hissed back

'Hi, there!' Jason's smile was broad and genuine. With very short cut hair, Jason was extremely good-looking. His black eyes sparkled with good humour. He was a bit taller than Dermot and Natalia, his tight shirt showing off an impressive physique. 'Mum's always talking about you, Natalia. Is this your husband? Hi, Dermot.'

'Jason's in the London Transport Police unit,' Natalia told Dermot, raising her voice as the volume of noise in the room increased as more of Rasheda's friends arrived, and Rasheda set some music playing quietly.

'Just passed my final exams. This party's a bit of a celebration.'

'Congratulations. Was it difficult?'

151

'You've got to do physical trainin' – that's OK 'cos I've always worked out – and then there's the written exams. You have to remember lots of legal stuff. Worst thing was giving up my ear studs though.'

'Where's your first assignment?' Dermot asked.

As they talked, Natalia noticed Rasheda coming round with wine to offer top ups. She went to help her. 'Your Jason is lovely,' she said. 'So full of enthusiasm. And so handsome.'

'He's a good boy. That Honey's good for him. About time he let someone take care of him. Feels he has to take care of us all ever since my husband–' Trailing off, Rasheda quickly recovered. 'Now don't tell him he's handsome or his head will get even bigger. I must tell him at least a dozen times a day,' Rasheda said, smiling. 'Now, if you can take this red round, I'll get another bottle of white, and I need a beer and a gin and tonic. I'm hoping people will start helping themselves soon.'

Natalia looked for a glass to fill and found herself confronting Avon.

'Hello, Avon. What an amazing dress,' she said as she poured the wine.

Her hair was still magenta, and she wore a Chinese-style top and skirt of a matching colour mixed with black that flared in and out over her ample curves.

'I got it in a sale at East, a couple of years ago. Liked those boots you wore yesterday. Harvey Nicks, if I'm not mistaken.'

'Um,' Natalia said, then decided to come clean. 'Hackney market, but label cut out, so they could be. Lots of bargains there. You must try it.'

'Maybe I will, but I live the other way, near West Hampstead.'

The two women looked at each other. Avon took a slurp of wine.

'Is Donna coming tonight?' Natalia thought of asking.

'She's got an important dinner.'

'Ah, mixing with the bigwigs again.'

'Mmm, and there's an added attraction. Some policeman she really fancies – Jonathan.'

Rasheda returned. The beer was for Mark, who was standing nearby, regaling two of Jason's friends about football. Leaning over, he gave Natalia's shrug a stroke. 'Is it still alive?' he joked. 'Should I call the RSPCA?'

Before Natalia could think of an answer, football claimed his attention again. She then saw Omar, standing with his wife near the archway that led to the kitchen. She approached them.

'Hello, Omar, and you must be Jamila. I'm Natalia. I've been working with your husband recently.'

His wife gave a sweet smile and murmured

153

a greeting.

With Omar simply nodding, Natalia felt rather foolish but persevered. 'I've seen your children – in the photograph on Omar's desk, they're gorgeous.'

'Thank you,' said Jamila shyly.

'Can I get you a drink? Or some nuts or crisps?'

'No, thank you,' said Omar. 'We have some water.'

'Oh, good.'

Nonplussed, Natalia looked round and was rescued by Rasheda.

'Can you help me in the kitchen?' she asked. 'Last-minute preparations.'

'Love to,' Natalia said, and followed her through, glad to escape from Omar's chilly presence.

15

'So come on, now I've got you on your own, tell me what you've seen on your secret tapes?' Rasheda asked. 'Did you spy on creepy Cliff up to no good? Or maybe somebody having a naughty snog? I'm dying to hear.'

In reply, Natalia looked round Rasheda's kitchen and said, 'This place looks like a bomb has exploded. How can you cook in here?'

Rasheda laughed. 'Oh, this is quite tidy for me. Come on, help me clear a space, so we can get the food on the table. Then people can help themselves, buffet style.'

The kitchen of Rasheda's flat was big, with the original wooden flooring sanded and varnished. In the centre was a huge farm-house table surrounded by a mixed collection of chairs. An old fireplace now held a big cooker, on which an array of pans were bubbling, the rising steam releasing wonderful spicy smells around the room. There were vases of all shapes and sizes, with dried flowers and real flowers, as well as baskets and paintings and photographs. But despite the size of the kitchen, every surface was covered with the plates, pots and cooking utensils Rasheda had used to create the meal. On the table was a set of brightly coloured bowls covered in cling film, containing a variety of salads.

Natalia and Rasheda rolled up their sleeves and began clearing away. From the living room, came the sound of music, and the laughter and conversation of the other guests.

'This room really seems to be you,' Natalia said. 'It's full of energy and life.'

'I do tend to live in the kitchen,' Rasheda agreed. 'But stop avoiding the issue and tell me about the tape. Oh, hold on a minute,' she said, wiping a hand across her brow. 'It's hot in here.' She went to open a small skylight window. 'Right, plates are in that dresser, and cutlery over there. Now, spill!'

'It was great news when Avon asked Omar to activate those two old CCTV cameras in the vault. That's one "special measure" of hers I approve of,' Natalia said. 'No one else knows except me, senior management and Omar – and now you. As I told you, one of them is positioned near the entrance to the Special Items room. Yesterday, I made regular checks on the footage from these two cameras. All day. Result?

'Very disappointing. I have nothing to report. I did not see anyone misbehaving, or looking suspicious. No diary. No shoes.'

'You really want to find that diary now, don't you?'

'You bet. Peter Bookman doesn't seem to know it's gone. At least, he never mentioned it. Supposing Helen wrote down where she was going on Friday? It would give us somewhere to start.'

Rasheda nodded. 'You need to nab that naughty hoaxer! And we still don't know what that "special" room is used for!'

'No.' Natalia had laid out plates and cutlery, napkins and condiments, and now began removing the cling film from the salads of fruits, nuts and vegetables. 'Cliff went in for a while and I'm sure he had a guilty expression when he came out. Stefan went in for about five minutes. He's not supposed to have a key, but I expect he borrowed Cliff's. Nobody else.'

'Ugh, that Cliff, he always stares through me. I did ask him to come tonight but he turned me down flat. Like, he's got such a busy social life, I don't think. Maybe he's a vampire out stalking his next victim!' she shuddered theatrically.

Natalia remembered the furtive look Cliff had given both ways when he'd come out of that room. 'Every time I begin to think he's OK, that people just misunderstand him, he goes all strange again. He could be the Hoaxer of course.'

'Maybe. The Hoaxer's gotta be someone in that office, and it ain't me and it ain't you. So ... had you considered Avon?'

'We must consider everyone, eliminate each possibility one by one, then what we have left must be the answer. Mark is already eliminated as the Hoaxer.' She glanced over her shoulder to make sure she couldn't be heard. A great burst of laughter came from the living room. 'Why do you think it might be Avon?'

'I think she makes too much of a song and dance about it. She protests too much. She's setting it up so's she can get lots of attention – then stops, and gets Brownie points from

Donna for stopping the Hoaxer.'

'It's a good theory. Oh, I don't know.' Jobs done, Natalia sank onto a kitchen chair. 'I'm beginning to think I should stop thinking about it, and leave the Hoaxer to Avon, and Helen Bookman to the police.'

'Here, let me fill your glass of wine and you can tell Auntie Rasheda all about it. The food can wait for five minutes. They're all having a good time getting sloshed in there. You look a bit down.'

Natalia took a gulp of wine. 'It's been a very up and down week. Not just the upset over Nuala's bullying on Thursday. Dermot went very quiet, instead of shouting at her, and that shook her even more. When he took Nuala back, he nearly shouted at Kathleen, which would have been a waste of time as she just shouts back. But he managed to stop himself and suggest a family meeting instead.' She fiddled with a serviette. 'It was seeing Peter Bookman in his office. I'd thought he was a gentleman, concerned for his wife ... and then he changed into this cold and angry person. It sounded as if ... as if he hated women. It was such a shock. It brought it all back to me.'

'Brought all what back?' Rasheda's voice held concern.

Natalia took a deep breath. She'd been wanting to confide in her friend, needing to share her feelings with someone. Dermot

158

knew and understood, but he was too deeply involved with her. Talking about it distressed him on her behalf. 'I was married before. Ten years ago. Jem is Turkish.' She smiled fleetingly. 'We were so in love. My family liked him, though his family, the ones in Poland, were not so keen on me. We worked hard. And we,' she swallowed hard, 'we had a child, a boy. My son. Paul.' It was a luxury to speak his name aloud, though he was in her thoughts every moment of the day. 'He's ... he's nine.'

'Oh, my dear.' Rasheda put her arm round her friend's shoulders and hugged her. 'Where is he now?'

'In Turkey. With his father. But I don't know exactly where. I haven't seen him or spoken to him for five years.' She took a ragged breath. 'Jem – took – him – from – me. It eats at me all the time. Jem's family wanted him to return home. He is the eldest son, you see. I didn't want to go. I didn't want to leave my family and my job. I thought Poland would offer Paul a good start in life. If we could've talked we could've worked something out but – Jem – he went mad. Every time the subject came up. Shouting and ... shoving me about. I became frightened of his anger, of what he might do. One night, I decided it was too much. When he fell asleep, I managed to escape with Paul and went to my parents' house.

'I didn't hear from him. Every day I went from fear that an angry Jem would turn up to longing for the sweet Jem I'd married. After a while, I began to feel that we were safe. I drove past our old house, but he wasn't living there any more.

'Then, one day, the kindergarten phoned. Jem had managed to snatch Paul from the playground. He'd had it all planned. They left Poland right away. I couldn't stop him.'

'Oh, honey, how terrible for you. Dermot knows?'

'Yes. He'd like us to have a baby together, but I ... I feel it would be a betrayal of Paul, at the moment. Dermot's been so supportive. Would you like to see my son?' She took a photo from her purse. Her son's clear, blue eyes gazed from a tanned face beneath a thatch of jet-black hair. Could she detect a slight sadness there, a longing for his mother?

'Great kid! But that's him now, right?'

'Last Christmas. Every year my sister-in-law – it must be her, we always got on – sends me a photo. No letter. No address. So I know he is well.

'I tried so hard to trace him. After all, that was my job in Poland. But the laws were not helpful and Jem was clever and covered his tracks so well. My lost baby.' She kissed the photo and put it away.

A slight sound from behind made them

look round. It was Omar. 'I came to find some lemonade,' he explained, the impervious set of his face and his dark eyes softening. 'I couldn't help overhearing some of your story. I'm so sorry, Natalia. This modern world – it's tearing our families apart.'

Natalia wiped her eyes as Rasheda got up to fetch another big bottle of lemonade. 'You sound as if you too have lost someone.'

'I have, but not as tragically as you. It's my brother. When we left Iran, the authorities would not let my brother come with us. He was made to go into the army.' He stopped. 'You saw his photograph, on my desk. That was us when we were growing up. We were very close.'

Natalia recalled the two carefree young men, arms around each other's shoulders. 'He did not want to join the army?'

'No. He's a journalist, and considered a possible subversive. Every time I see a news story about Iranian activities, or that America might invade, I worry about him. And the Iranian government keep an eye on their exiles, skilled ones like me anyway. I feel I have to keep a low profile, for his sake and the rest of our family.'

'The worry is with you all the time.'

'That's right. I dread the knock upon the door. Natalia, you know I will do everything I can to help your search for this missing woman, Helen Bookman. You mustn't give up on her, just as you haven't given up on your son.'

'Thank you. I–'

'Hey, Mum, what's happened to the food? I'm starving. I told Mark you're the best cook, too. So where is it?' Jason burst in, followed by Mark and Stefan.

'Hungry boys to feed, I know how to do that. It's all ready, help yourselves. Natalia, you put the dressing on the salads...'

There was goat stew, chicken jerk, plantains – Rasheda had plundered her Caribbean heritage for a mix of spicy, fruity flavours.

Conversation died down as plates were loaded, glasses filled, and food began to be eaten. Omar returned to Jamila in the living room with two platefuls of salad and rice, as they were vegetarians, and there they talked with Rasheda's friends and neighbours. Avon gingerly picked out only those things she recognised, not willing to experiment. She followed the young men – Mark, Stefan and Jason and his two friends – to one corner of the big kitchen table, where she listened to them talking. They'd moved on from sport to action movies.

Natalia and Dermot sat at the other end of the table, with Rasheda and her downstairs neighbours. 'I want to try everything,' Natalia told them, while Dermot said, 'This goat stew is fantastic.'

Rasheda's younger son, Daniel, sat quietly

nearby soaking up all the adult talk. It brought back memories of family meals together back home. Gradually, Natalia felt the knots inside her untie and slip away.

Ice creams followed the main meal and then Stefan asked, 'Can I smoke by this little kitchen window, if I blow the smoke out. It's raining and cold outside.'

'Oh, go on, but if the smoke blows in, you go out!'

Stefan grinned and leaned as close to the window as he could. Natalia saw he smoked very low-tar cigarettes and barely dragged on them at all.

'Careful of your smoke,' Daniel suddenly said. 'Or my brother will arrest you.'

'Oi!' Jason said. 'As a London Transport policeman, fully fledged, I can tell people off for smoking, for putting their feet on seats – and for being cheeky, like you. So watch it.'

'Yeah, you on the white man's time, OK,' Daniel retorted.

Before Jason could give as good as he got, Rasheda swiped at Daniel with a tea towel. 'We don't have that sort of talk in this house, young man. And you should be proud of your brother.'

'Sorry, Mum.' Daniel was contrite. 'Shall I collect up the plates and put them in the dishwasher?'

'Yes, please.' Rasheda gave him a quick smile, which he returned. 'Let's all go in the living room and get some dancing going.' She ignored the protests and led the way, pretending to salsa as she went.

Natalia spotted that there was an ice cream tub still out, starting to melt. 'I'll just put this away,' she said to Jason.

'The freezer's out here.' He led her to a small utility room where there was an upright fridge freezer. In the middle of the fridge door was a photograph. A smiling man with dreadlocks was sitting on the grass, a boy on either side.

'That's my dad,' Jason said.

'He doesn't live here with you?'

Jason burst out laughing. 'He doesn't live anywhere, on the whole. He stops with various friends, does deals on the streets. Sometimes he gets a free bed and meals courtesy of Her Majesty's government, if you know what I mean. The local plod – uh, police – usually turn a blind eye to his ganja dealing. He and Mum were never officially married.' He took the ice cream and put it in the freezer below. 'I think she's still got a soft spot for him.'

'Wash your mouth out, chile.' Rasheda had found them. 'That man is nothing but trouble. Stop skulking out here.' As Natalia passed her she said softly, 'I'm glad you know. I was going to tell you about him.'

Natalia had an inkling that Jason was right about his mother.

164

16

Monday did not start auspiciously. Dermot couldn't find the shirt he wanted, and rain gusted from a very grey sky. A passing car swished through a puddle, sending cold, dirty water over Natalia's legs on the one day she wasn't wearing either boots or trousers. She'd chosen to wear a knee-length skirt and thick, black tights, and now the tights clung damply to her legs all the way to work. More worryingly, Homeless Joe was missing. She hoped that he was sheltering from the rain or had gone to the café already for his morning 'cuppa'. But his absence unsettled her.

One by one, Natalia's colleagues struggled in, shaking off the rain and grumbling about the weather. One or two were snuffling with colds. However, she did sense a friendlier atmosphere. Rasheda's party had helped break down some barriers. Avon for once was not standing frowning by her desk with her watch in her hand checking whether anyone was late. Instead, she was chatting with Stefan, who had casually sat on her desk. Natalia remembered her salsa'ing with Jason, swaying and dipping to the music, her inhibitions peeled away.

Even though Cliff had given her a lecture last week about channels and protocols away from the office, these English people had been relaxed in each other's company. All except for Cliff himself, who had refused Rasheda's invitation. Why was that, what were these meetings he mysteriously hurried off to in the evenings? Surely not speed dating, or lonely hearts' clubs. Perhaps he was learning to ballroom dance – or maybe he went to Alcoholics Anonymous?

The raindrops seemed to roll off Donna's raincoat as she came in. She removed it to reveal her smartest, most conservative trouser suit and crisp white shirt, with minimal make-up. She had her sleek, blonde hair smoothed back in its French pleat in a second, flashing nails that were expertly French polished. Natalia could not tell from her demeanour if things had worked out with her sexy policeman on Saturday night or not.

'No legs today, Donna?' Stefan called. 'Shame!'

Mark sauntered in last, whistling cheerfully. He stopped by Natalia's desk. 'Good party Saturday night – the bits I can remember!'

'Want to know what you and Avon got up to?'

'Was that before or after I started singing?' He grinned. 'Not on your way downstairs?'

'In a minute. I just wanted to check my

old desk.'

'I miss having a laugh with you.'

'Me, too. It's quite gloomy down there. Were you out at the football yesterday?'

'Me and the lads had a knockabout in the park, then we went down the pub. This geezer, he was in a right two and eight 'cos we wanted to cop a different match on the box,' he said, teasing her by putting on the cockney patter.

'Hmmm. I think I understand. We had a lovely family day – but I'm allowed because I'm nearly forty.'

They had spent a relaxing Sunday morning in bed, with late breakfast and the Sunday papers, half listening to the Archers on the radio. By lunchtime, their hangovers had gone and they picked up the children and took them to the Natural History Museum, where Connor loved the dinosaurs and even Nuala deigned to be distracted by the interactive wildlife displays. Although they circled each other gingerly, and Nuala still looked surly, outright warfare did not break out.

In the evening, she and Dermot went to see an Irish band play in a local pub. Peter Bookman had not called her over the weekend, nor were there any news bulletins about him, or his missing wife. She began to think that Dermot was right. She should step aside and leave it to the professionals.

167

Natalia had decided to see if she could catch Cliff and suggest that, if he did find Helen's missing shoes, surely now a low priority, he should take them to the police, not bring them to her. Cliff did not appear, however, so she headed downstairs. Would today be less gloomy now Omar had thawed towards her? Once again, he had arrived early and was sitting studying the CCTV already. However, he looked up when she went in, smiling warmly.

'Hello, Natalia, ready to do some snooping?'

'Ah, I prefer to think of it as sleuthing,' she smiled.

By tacit agreement, neither mentioned the private revelations they'd shared on Saturday night. But as the morning went on, Omar did spend time passing on some of his expert knowledge to her. She sympathised even more at his frustration in being forced to go over and over old tapes in a search for the Shoe Fetishist, when he'd rather be looking for more meaningful incidents.

Natalia also spent some time in the fruitless search for the Shoe Fetishist, then she moved over to the CCTV footage of the LPO office for the weekend. This was particularly dull. Watching the screen, not even a mouse stirred in the vault. She moved on to Monday morning and started to frown. Something wasn't right.

She ran forward and back on the tape. The camera that covered the area near the Special Items room was showing a very blurred image.

'Omar, what do you make of this?'

'Looks like it's slipped position, and is showing us a blank, out-of-focus wall.'

'Shall I go and check it?'

'Go ahead. Cliff can reach it with his step-ladders, or call me if there are any problems.'

For the first time, Natalia signed herself into the vault. She could hear voices and footsteps in the distance. She hoped she would remember the way from last Wednesday night. First the umbrellas, then the shoes. She hesitated. Was it left or right here? She tried to the right but soon realised she was going the wrong way and turned back. Once again she felt uncertain until she turned a corner, and there was the cornucopia of children's pencil cases and lunchboxes.

The colours clashed violently with Avon's hair, which was raven's-wing black this week. She must do it on Sunday evenings, Natalia decided, visualising her sitting in a fluffy robe, towel round her head, Kleenex and chocolates to hand, watching a weepy girlie film.

But what was Avon doing? She had her back to Natalia, and was unaware of her. She was reaching boxes from the shelf, opening them, looking inside, then replacing them.

What was she looking for? All traces of food were removed before storage.

At the moment she reached Avon, she saw an open box in her hand. Inside the box was a pair of tan-leather high heels. They looked very much like Helen Bookman's shoes. In the next moment she became aware of Natalia, and whirled round.

'What are you doing here?' Avon demanded, face and neck turning bright red. As ever, attack was her usual form of defence.

'I've come to adjust the CCTV camera. It's either slipped position, or someone has tampered with it.'

'Well, it wasn't me.' Avon was trying to replace the lid on the box.

'I didn't say it was. But I want to look at those shoes. Why are you hiding them?'

'Because ... because I like them.'

'They're too big for you.'

'I can put insoles in them. You don't think I can afford designer shoes like this on my salary do you?'

Natalia glanced at the lunchboxes. 'Are there more shoes in there?'

'Might be.' Avon stood her ground. 'Maybe one or two. Anyway, what's it got to do with you? You were the one who gave away those Jimmy Choos. I had to do something to keep the shoes I really want. And if someone ever had come in to claim them, then they would have mysteriously shown up.'

'So it's my fault now! Look, Avon, I think those are the shoes that belong to the missing woman, Helen Bookman. You remember the handbag and the diary?'

Avon looked sadly down at the lunchbox, knowing she was going to have to lose these shoes, too. 'I thought as she was missing, no one would want the shoes. After all, they can't help find her, can they?'

'I don't know. We should let her husband or the police decide that.'

'Oh, very well. Here you are. Another pair of shoes you've done me out of.' She thrust the box ungraciously at Natalia and stomped off.

'Come to Hackney market,' Natalia called after her. 'Designer goods, affordable prices!'

She peeled off the lunchbox lid and looked at the pair of shoes nestling toe to heel in there. She was sure now that Avon could not be the Hoaxer. Her only interest was in designer labels.

Carefully she stood the shoes up in the box. Avon was probably right, the shoes would give nothing away about what had happened to Helen. Suddenly, she stiffened and looked closer. There, on the inside rim of both shoes, were the dark, rust-coloured stains of what could only be blood.

17

Natalia awoke with a start the next day. She'd been dreaming, she couldn't quite remember what it was about, but the dream had been full of looming shapes and she'd been filled with dread. Immediately, she remembered what had been preying on her mind: the bloodstained shoes.

Overnight, Natalia had locked the shoes in her desk drawer because though she had phoned the police station handling the Bookman case in Swiss Cottage, and left two messages, no one had called her back. She had puzzled endlessly on her way home over the stains on the shoes. There could be so many rational explanations. But her mind insisted on coming up with sinister ones. How much was that to do with her own past, and how much with the reality of the Bookman's relationship?

And now it was another commute to work. The everydayness of her journey began to wear away the unwelcome thoughts from her sleeping mind. But then, in the middle of the rushing crowds at Baker Street, she had an overpowering sensation that she was being followed. She stopped and stepped to one side. Pupils from a local convent school passed by, wearing their distinctive green uniforms and hats, followed by Japanese tourists, cameras ready for when they reached Baker Street and caught their first glimpse of the Sherlock Holmes Museum at the mythical 221B Baker Street. They did not even seem to see her, let alone be watching her.

Natalia looked back towards the ticket barriers, then around at the shop fronts. She found she was searching for someone hiding their face in a newspaper or observing her by looking in a mirror. 'Too many James Bond movies,' she told herself. Dermot and Connor loved to watch them together.

Then she saw the CCTV cameras. Of course, that had to be it. None of the passers-by was paying her any attention. She almost waved to the cameras, which would, at the moment, be waving to herself. Now she was one of the watchers, rather than the watched.

It was one of those oddities about England she quietly enjoyed. The native people prided themselves on their freedoms, maintaining their own constitution, driving on the 'wrong' side of the road, keeping the British pound. An Englishman's home is his castle on which he generally pulls up the drawbridge. She'd learned early on that you had to be invited in, not drop round when you felt like it.

And yet English people were surely the most spied upon in Europe. Cameras of all types watched their every move. Computers tracked their every transaction. Mostly they accepted it as being for the common good, but Natalia felt uneasy at times. She'd been born in 1970, when Poland was behind the Iron Curtain, and the communist regime had regulated their lives with minute attention to detail. Her parents had protected her from this knowledge as much as they could, but she'd still been aware of it.

'This is for you.'

Natalia smiled in relief. Homeless Joe was back in his rightful place. He was holding out the morning *Metro* to her, one of London's three free newspapers.

'Thank you,' she said, handing him the customary coin. 'Where were you yesterday?'

''Ospital. Me 'ead.' He lifted some of his matted hair and Natalia saw a neat sticking plaster. 'Couple of yobs took a dislike to me, see. I should find them and thank them. Nice bed for the night and lots of tea. Even got me feet looked at as well.' But he was still wearing the same ancient battered trainers with the soles flapping loose. Pity the hospital hadn't been able to give him new shoes.

She instinctively glanced over to the spot where she'd first seen Peter Bookman pasting the picture of his wife, exactly one week ago. It was covered now with legitimate posters. 'Shoe sculpture' she read. Underneath, sculpted into the form of a woman, were hundreds of high-heeled shoes. I wonder how the sculptor managed that, she thought, pausing momentarily to admire their expertise. There was such a kaleidoscope of colours and sizes, but making a harmonious whole, and all of them sexy high heels. I wonder, she thought.

Natalia paused at the entrance to the LPO. There it was again. A primeval itch between her shoulder blades. Was she being followed? Slowly and deliberately, she looked up the street towards Regent's Park, then down towards Baker Street station and the massive traffic jam that was Marylebone High Street. Opposite the awnings flapped on the scaffolding that covered the Art Deco building opposite the LPO office. However she could not see anyone observing her, or indeed pretending not to observe her.

She collected a cup of coffee and took it down to the CCTV room, still with the *Metro* tucked under her arm. For once, Omar was not there before her. She opened up, put on the lights, set the old Cona machine working. She switched on her computer, then sat down to drink her coffee and glance at the paper while the PC was booting up.

It didn't take her long to track down the name of the artist, Sharon Mirza, a traditional Turkish name in a traditionally Muslim country. Could it be? It didn't take Natalia long to locate a photograph of Mrs Mirza, who was something of a non-conformist, not being one to adhere to traditional garb. Seeing that, Natalia wondered if she was heading off on the wrong track, but something made her persevere.

When Omar came in, she was diligently poring over footage of the barriers at Holborn tube station, the closest stop to Ms Mirza's art gallery, alongside documented evidence of every time the Shoe Fetishist had struck. Pausing the footage for the third time, she saw a woman in a burqa exiting through the barriers at Holborn tube. The times all coincided with a robbery, and still gave her time to get from the scene of the crime and back to Holborn. But why?

'Good morning, Natalia,' Omar said in his usual quiet manner. Since Rasheda's party, however, his iciness had completely gone. 'I'm sorry to be late. Thank you for opening up.'

'I'm glad you've arrived. It's a bit spooky down here all by myself. But I think I may have found something.'

'Yes?'

'The Shoe Fetishist. I think I may have found her.'

Natalia could not conceal her elation. For the next hour, the pair bent over the computer screen, examining the footage, and at long last Omar pushed back in his swivel chair, stood up and began pacing.

'We'll never be able to prove it beyond reasonable doubt, of course, but there's enough circumstantial evidence. That, combined with the fact that there have been no reports of stolen footwear in the past week, and I suspect there won't be again; I do believe, Mrs Dermot, you've solved the crime.' Omar clapped her on the back.

'I couldn't have done it without you, Watson,' Natalia joked, to which Omar smiled broadly. 'Why do you think she did it though?'

'I'm sure if you headed along to her art show, there would be some clue,' Omar said.

'Ah, I think this is one crime I can leave well alone. At least this will make Avon happy. Now I guess it's just the Hoaxer left, and then I'll be out of your hair.'

'Ah, I need to talk to you about that. Let me get some coffee first.'

Mug in hand, Omar swivelled his chair round to face her. 'There's a new head of operations. It seems I'm needed back at CCTV headquarters. It's near Bank, as I think you know. I am going to have to leave you.'

'Oh.' Natalia was touched by sadness at the thought of him going. 'Will it mean more responsibility again for you though?'

There was a sudden twinkle in Omar's eye. 'It seems I am to be trusted after all. I think it's time I proved just how good I am, don't you? You'll be working here alone, but you can call me if you've got any questions. If you find it too difficult by yourself, I'll tell Donna to close this station down.'

'Thanks. When will you be leaving?'

'Tomorrow, I'm afraid,' he said gently. 'But I hope we'll keep in touch. Jamila wants to invite you and Dermot round some time.'

'We'd like that.'

Natalia started her viewing again. She found she had less enthusiasm for her task, now she knew Omar would be moving on. Though he'd been slow to open up at first, over the last two days she'd learned that the austere façade he presented to the world enclosed a man of stoicism and hidden wisdom.

His childhood in rural Iran, as one of seven children, he recalled as idyllic: *If only you had seen our house, Natalia, surrounded by mulberry and walnut trees, you would have sworn you were in Eden*. But with hindsight, Omar recognised his parents must have sheltered him and his siblings from the political unrest that would come to fracture the country.

In the 70s, when he was a teenager with aspirations to study mechanical engineering and join the ranks of educated Iranians working with foreign oil companies, the growing problems with inflation meant that his family, relatively wealthy though they were, began to struggle financially. *My mother hadn't worked until then, you understand. My father's doctor's salary was enough.* Eventually, she took a job as a teacher, joking that bringing up Omar and his brothers and sisters was more than adequate training.

When Natalia asked about his marriage to Jamila, he had clammed up for a few minutes, and she wondered if she had offended him with such a personal question. She filled the gap with her own story about meeting Dermot in Poland, and found that even now the memory of his boyish Irish face set her heart aflutter. Omar had listened attentively, and when her tale was over, described his time at the Amirkabir University of Technology in Tehran. Jamila was a lab assistant there. Natalia noticed the inadvertent smile that crept over his normally severe lips when he mentioned their first meeting. The local cinema was showing *Dirty Dancing,* and Jamila found his impersonation of Patrick Swayze's dancing endearing, even if lamentably bad. Their groups of friends had mixed well, and several lasting romances had blossomed between Omar's student buddies and her circle.

But then he felt the devastating force of the Ayatollah's hand personally. He recalled his mother being forced from her job with the Ayatollah's strict edicts on gender roles, and his father being subject to reprisals not for something he said, but for the liberal views he was suspected of harbouring. Natalia didn't push for details, but was told anyway that his father died in the early 80s.

Omar abandoned his studies and fled with Jamila to England as soon as possible after that. *Iran was no longer my country*. The young couple were married in a Mosque in Willesden, and rented a tiny flat in nearby Stonebridge Park. Full of hope, and eager to continue his degree, he'd suffered the indignity of being turned away because of his poor English. *I have never felt so powerless to express myself,* he told her.

'But you fought back,' said Natalia. 'That's what matters.'

'Perhaps,' he'd replied, but from his tone, she knew there was still a bitterness that rankled deep within. And who could blame him? As Omar left that day, Natalia found herself grateful that he was letting her, whose struggles seemed minor in comparison, into his life.

She watched as Cliff did a complete circuit of his kingdom first thing in the morning, coughing as he went. She shook her head. She hoped he would give up smoking one of these days! He carefully checked that the Special Items room was locked. She was now watching in real time. It felt odd to be

180

sitting here, spying on her colleagues.

She found herself keeping a special eye out for Avon. Ever since she'd caught her squirreling away designer shoes, Avon had avoided her, whereas before she'd never missed an opportunity to boss her about. Every time she passed a CCTV camera she squinted up as if she expected to see Natalia's eyes framed in the camera lens, and then she'd toss her head defiantly and bustle on her way.

At last it was lunchtime. 'OK if I go now?' Natalia asked.

Omar nodded. 'Jamila has made my lunch for me again,' he said. 'I'll go out for a walk when you get back.'

'Thanks. I've got to make a start on my Christmas shopping. My relatives have sent me their wish lists. I'm going to have to go to Harrods in Knightsbridge, Fortnum and Mason in Piccadilly, and of course Marks and Spencer. But today it's the British Library.'

As Natalia arrived upstairs, Donna was coming out of her office waving some papers above her head. Today her hair was down, loosely bouncing on her shoulders, and the red of her tight, short skirt matched the red of her lipstick.

'Gather round, everyone.' She announced loudly, heading for the noticeboard. 'It's time we had a team-building exercise. Stop groaning, whoever that was. I want to make sure we're well bonded and ready to respond to any questions when the inspector arrives. We must win that title from Manchester.'

She was pinning up the sheets on the board, beside the poster of Helen Bookman, and another new one, also signed by Donna, requesting volunteers to train for the London Marathon.

'Two-thirty sharp this afternoon in the boardroom upstairs. Don't be late.'

'What do we have to do?' Avon had thrust herself to the front and was peering at the paper.

'Role-playing exercises, so we can learn about each others' jobs, and the customers' problems, too. You change partners every ten minutes, and I've listed some roles we can assume, or situations we might encounter.'

'I'm not partnering Cliff,' Avon muttered. 'He smells like an ashtray.'

'You won't have to,' Cliff's voice came from the back. 'I'll be down here keeping an eye on everything while you're playing upstairs.'

Natalia glanced at her watch. She'd have to hurry if she was going to get her shopping done, and then return in time to prepare for the exercise.

As she left, she thought that although he tried to hide it, she'd heard the hurt in Cliff's voice. Avon must be especially sensitive to smells, she thought. Like Great Uncle Jan's pipe tobacco, Cliff's cigarettes had an almost sweet smell. But also like Great Uncle Jan, could his hard exterior hide a soft centre?

18

Natalia emerged out of Euston underground station and headed towards the soaring gothic towers of the newly refurbished St Pancras, London's rail gateway to Paris and beyond. The roaring traffic in the Euston Road was the same traffic that struggled past Baker Street.

The area around King's Cross and St Pancras was being beautified and brought into the twenty-first century at incredible speed, but even so there were architectural miracles from the past going largely un-noticed; cupolas and statues graced buildings in need of restoration.

She wasn't going as far as that though. Before she reached St Pancras she turned through the redbrick walls that fronted Euston Road into the concrete piazza of the British Library. Her studious niece Anna was in her second year at Krakow University and had begged her to pick up leaflets and information. She hoped to register to use its facilities via the Internet.

Natalia crossed the open square, noting the Christmas tree had been put up, ready to receive its lights, and the few brave souls sitting at tables outside the piazza café. On the wide, shallow steps leading to the library entrance, she paused and looked beck, having once again that overwhelming sensation that she was being followed. Did someone just dodge behind a pillar? She waited. But no one emerged. She really was feeling spooked today. She hurried on in.

After picking up Anna's leaflets and spending half an hour browsing through the shop and buying some Christmas cards and books as presents, marvelling at the treasure trove of literature and ancient manuscripts that were housed in and beneath this building, Natalia's stomach was protesting at the lack of food. She had a few minutes to spare to buy a sandwich and drink at the café, which fortunately had inside tables, too.

Natalia halted at the entrance, and looked at one of the tables outside. A man was sitting there, hiding behind a newspaper. She walked over and pulled it down. She was right. It was Peter Bookman. They stared at one another. Her heart stood still for a second. It could not be a coincidence.

'You have been following me all day,' she

said firmly, brooking no denial. 'Why?'

His face was a mask of misery. The shadows under his eyes were darker, his attempts at shaving clumsier. His once-smart city suit and overcoat were even more dishevelled than before.

'I had to,' he said. 'I had to find out.'

'Find out what?' she demanded. 'I come to you in good faith, I offer my help...What are you doing?'

'That's just it. I want to find out what *you're* doing.'

'I'm not doing anything. I–'

He stood up quickly, careless of the chair tumbling over behind him. 'You know, don't you. You know where Helen is. You planned this together, making that CCTV tape to confuse me. That's the only explanation.'

Natalia gave a snort of disbelief. 'Don't be ridiculous. I work in lost property, like I told you. You only have to ring to check that out. And I only started doing CCTV work last Wednesday, you ask my boss.'

Peter Bookman stepped towards her and gripped her arm. 'They'll lie to protect you. Maybe they even helped you. I can't get my head around that tape. That's not Helen, leaving her things on the train on purpose. I won't believe it.' He shook his head as if to clear it.

'It's crazy, following me.'

'I thought if I followed you, perhaps you

would lead me to her. So I waited at Baker Street, where we first met.' He grabbed her by both arms now and thrust his face into hers. 'You've got to tell me – where are you hiding her?' He was practically shaking Natalia now. A vision of the bloodied shoes flashed into her mind. Just what was this man capable of? 'Or have you been feeding her tablets, drugging her?'

'Mr Bookman! Stop this at once. I have not kidnapped your wife. I've never met her. Now, let me go.' She was aware of bystanders watching to see if she needed help.

'You were asking about her tablets, in my office,' he was saying, his fingers pressing painfully into her arms. 'I found out she got extra ones – she got a repeat prescription. They wouldn't agree to more. You could be sedating her. It's the only explanation I can think of for why she won't come home to me.'

'I can think of another.' Natalia looked him squarely in the eye. 'We just found her shoes. And they're covered in blood.'

Then Peter released her, guilt and shame chasing across his face. 'Her shoes? How could they... Oh, I remember, she cut her foot. That morning – the last time I saw her.'

'Why didn't you mention this before?'

'She put a plaster on before putting on her shoes. It must've come off. It didn't seem important. But maybe you already know that. Very convenient, finding her shoes just now.'

'Do you realise you sound completely paranoid.'

They stared at one another. At last Peter Bookman hung his head. 'I know, I know,' he mumbled. 'Saying it out loud just now, I can see it sounds crazy. The thing is, I feel as if I *am* going crazy. I can't make sense of anything, my whole world is turned upside down, and you ... you get these strange thoughts. They're like hallucinations, till you don't know what's real and what you've dreamed.'

'Her medication. You know I only heard about it when your mother-in-law phoned you, and then you said that the tablets were mild. But now you're worried she's got a repeat prescription. Why is that? Does Helen suffer from more than feeling just "low"? Does she have depression?'

'No, yes ... yes, all right, she was de-pressed... But wouldn't you be? Going through what she went through. What we *both* went through.'

Natalia tensed. This was it, this was what he'd been hiding from her. 'Going through?' she questioned.

Peter Bookman forced the words out unwillingly. 'It's the longing, every month. Riding the rollercoaster of hope, then disappointment, over and over again.'

'Ah.' Light dawned. 'Every month. You both wanted a baby?'

He choked on the words. 'Helen – couldn't – conceive.'

'Come inside,' she ordered. 'I'll get us some coffee and then you will tell me exactly what happened the Friday Helen went.'

'The baby?' she prompted him when they were sitting down, two cappuccinos in front of them.

'We longed for a child,' his voice sounded very far away. All the fight seemed to have left him now his secret was out in the open. 'Only it didn't happen. A year, two, three went by and then we decided to get tested, follow the doctor's advice.' Peter drank some of the coffee. 'I could see it was taking a terrible toll on Helen. She felt she was failing in some way. When I said I didn't mind, she felt I was belittling her emotions.'

Natalia nodded. 'I have a friend, Marta, in Poland. She went through this. No one can really understand the terrible longing, the hope, and then the loss of hope.'

'That's exactly it. So we applied for IVF. We couldn't get it on the NHS, something about lack of quota in our area. We went private. Had to work all hours to pay for it. Again, we had disappointment after disappointment. And then because you can't bear it, you start blaming each other. We would fall apart, and then come back together again.'

188

'And that Friday morning you were falling apart again.'

He sat in silence for a moment, turning the foam over and over in his cup with a teaspoon. Then he spoke in a dull monotone. 'We argued that morning. A really blazing row that came out of nowhere. I don't know what made it happen. Before I knew it, we were yelling at each other. And then it happened.'

Natalia hardly dared breath. Was this the moment of confession?

'Helen picked up a vase – it was a lovely crystal vase, a wedding present – and threw it at me. Glass and water and flowers everywhere.' He gave a dry laugh. 'Almost like she wanted to smash our marriage like she smashed the vase. That's how it felt to me. Like a blow to the heart.' He looked up at her. 'That's when she cut her foot, when we were picking up the glass. She blamed me for that. But then she quietened down.'

Natalia absorbed this further insight into Helen. 'And then you left for work.'

'That's right. The last thing she said to me was what did I want for supper.'

'You've given all these details to the police?'

'Of course. But I didn't want the whole world knowing our private business because Helen made me promise not to tell anyone about our IVF treatment, not even her mother. She didn't want to go through the

189

endless questioning, over and over. But it did, in the end, weigh on her mind.' He stood up wearily. 'I have to go now. The shoes – do what you will with them.'

'Peter?' Natalia called out after him, as he was halfway across the piazza.

'Yes?' He answered, turning.

'Can you think why Helen would have had trainers with her that day?"

'No. She wasn't heading into work, and that's the only time she carried them. When she was heading into Canary Wharf.'

Not knowing what to make of that, Natalia merely thanked him and stared down at her empty coffee cup after he'd gone. She had held out a helping hand to Peter, but he was afraid to take it, afraid to trust her. And now she did not know what to trust. Her own instincts or the mounting evidence against Peter. Was it Helen who wanted to keep their childlessness secret – or was it Peter? What could she believe? That Helen and Peter loved each other but, tormented by their inability to have a child, they'd had a terrible row and later Helen walked out, presumably to cool off ... and then what? She only had Peter's word for that.

Or was this just one incident of many when Peter had physically attacked his wife. He was a control freak, using Natalia to track down his wife who had finally escaped, just as she, Natalia, had. Wanting to drag Helen back into his abusive power again, perhaps belittling her for her childlessness. No wonder she became depressed.

Natalia shivered. She was as committed as ever to the search for the lost woman, but now it was entirely for Helen's sake.

19

'This is not a good start,' Donna said, looking pointedly at her watch. 'The meeting was supposed to start at two-thirty and it's twenty-five to three already.'

She began to pace up and down in front of the table on which lay piles of A4 paper. A whiteboard had also been set up, on which various diagrams had already been sketched in black pen. Avon sat right at the front, eagerly waiting to prove herself to her boss, pen poised above a new pad of paper. She had been first to arrive.

Natalia heard the door creak open. 'Thank you for joining us, Mark. You've kept all your work mates waiting. I think we can take this as our first lesson. Consideration for your colleagues.'

'Sorry, everyone. Footie results, from Australia. Big black mark to me.' Mark was irrepressible.

'Very well, we accept your apology.' Donna took charge, cutting Avon off. 'Now onto business. My father always said you can't go into battle with your army half trained, so this is about training. But we're doing it the easy way, by playing. Role-playing. First of all, I want you to team up with the person sitting next to you.

'Then I'm going to hand out paper on which will be written your role, so whatever you get, it'll be quite random. After ten minutes, we'll switch partners and take on new roles. It should be a useful learning experience. I'd like to draw your attention first of all to this diagram here.' She turned and then did a double take on seeing what had been drawn on the board.

'Right, no prizes for guessing who might be responsible for showing us the classic two-two-four attacking formation in football,' she swung back. But it appeared nothing was going to ruffle her good humour, as she wore a broad grin. 'OK, let's get to it.'

Still recovering from her encounter with Peter Bookman, Natalia was glad her first partner was Mark. He'd help take her mind off things for a while.

'I'm an embarrassed customer in reception,' Natalia said. 'Who are you?'

'I'm Cliff!'

'Remember, people, have fun with this but take it seriously, too,' Donna called out.

'The purpose of the game is to identify areas where we fall down, and why, and how we can improve upon them in future. Begin please.'

'Um,' Natalia began, addressing Mark/ Cliff, 'I'm rather embarrassed but I left something of a rather personal nature on the bus.'

'Now what might that be? Underwear? Birth-control pills? Those little rubbery things you women stuff down your bras. Now we have a whole area dedicated to those things. Slippery as eels, some of them.'

'Mark!'

'No, no, it's Cliff,' he grinned. 'You know it's true. The man would reel off a list until he got it right, while the woman would be backing away outside, and still he'd be following her, down the street, insisting that he could find the offending item, priding himself on his ability to track down anything, even if he has nothing more to go on than that. And lord help the woman if she's foreign. He'd be shouting at her all the way down Euston Road.'

'Donna?' Avon's voice rose above the din in the room. 'I don't think Mark and Natalia are taking this seriously.'

'Ah, lassie,' Mark responded in his best faux Scottish accent. 'We all canna take things as seriously as you.'

'Maybe it's time we changed partners

then,' was Donna's solution, smoothing over the incident. Natalia had to give Donna credit. She was a born diplomat.

Natalia's next partner was Donna's secretary, Rose.

'Hello, Rose. Welcome back. How was your holiday? Is this your first day back?'

'It is and, thank you, it was very good. I was on a spiritual retreat in Scotland.' Rose, a quiet, plain girl, who wore a gold cross on a chain round her neck, smiled, which transformed her into almost pretty. 'I've got to be an angry customer.'

'And I've got to be Avon. Now how shall I play that?'

'I think you'll find it easy to provoke me. Just don't listen to anything I say and then boss me about.'

They exchanged impish smiles.

'Donna must be glad to have you back.'

'She seems to have managed fine without me, and she's looking very glamorous again today, isn't she? She was starting to dress up a bit again before I went away. I hope she's met a new man. The last one went off with someone much younger, who was a model. Her ego was very bruised.'

They glanced sympathetically at Donna, who felt their gaze and looked back, raising an eyebrow.

'Uh oh, better get on with our role playing!'

Very soon, as Rose predicted, they were snapping at each other, with Rose giving as good as she got, even standing up and stamping her foot.

'Thank you,' Rose said afterwards. 'I found an assertive side I didn't even know I had.'

After a session with Jim, a steady, middle-aged man, she consulted her list, but before she could even read it, Avon bustled over. 'Here's your role,' she told Natalia. 'I'm Donna.'

'And I'm a customer with a disability.'

Natalia felt that Avon was still Avon, not Donna, and she was relieved when it was time for the last rotation.

She should have been partnered by Stefan, but he was nowhere to be seen. As each pair chose a corner of the room to work in, Natalia lingered near the door. If Donna noticed, she could always say he was a customer about to come in.

At last he slipped through the door of the boardroom. 'Sorry, Natalia, I was quick as I could be. What am I this time? Am I playing Avon?' He batted his eyelashes. 'Or Donna?' He mimed cracking a whip.

'Stop fooling about!' Natalia said. 'For this one you must be me and I must be you.'

'That's like a woman trying to lead a man in dancing. You end up going backwards. Much better, you speak Polish, I speak

Serbian and no one will know who is who.'

Ignoring him, Natalia went ahead with, 'I'm so tired. I only had two hours' sleep. The girls would not let me leave the club.'

'Be quiet, Stefan, I am trying to work here. I have serious things on my mind,' he paused. 'You do, Natalia. I've noticed, especially this last few days.'

'It's the missing woman, Helen Bookman,' she told him. 'And now I'm really worried that she might be in a very bad state of mind, perhaps even thinking of harming herself. I've found out that she has every good reason to be genuinely depressed – and before she disappeared, she got hold of an extra prescription of her antidepressant tablets.'

'Perhaps she was planning to leave the husband, and made sure she had enough to last her before she settle somewhere new?' Stefan suggested.

Natalia remembered how she had left Jem. There had been no time to organise anything. A flight to safety, that had been the only thing on her mind. 'True. Or maybe she could not bear her life any more and did not want him to try and stop her once she'd made up her mind.' Had that been the decision she'd made there, in that Circle Line carnage? 'But then that may be what her husband wants me to think, that she is unstable, to cover his own tracks. He can be very rough. Who knows what he might be capable of?' Unconsciously, she rubbed her upper arms where he'd seized her.'

'Don't worry, Natalia. No one has found a body. If anyone can work out where she is, it will be you. You are expert.' He laid a hand over hers and gave it a brotherly squeeze of comfort. Just as Avon walked by. 'Hmmph,' was all she said.

'If only I could work out who the Hoaxer is, and get them to tell me where they've put Helen's diary. I must just make some progress.'

'Thank you, everyone. Time's up.' Donna announced. 'You've worked hard and deserve a break. I'll just go to the executive kitchen and let the staff know we're ready for the refreshments I've arranged. I'm very pleased with this afternoon's work.'

Before long, tea trolleys were wheeled in, piled high with plates of biscuits, cups and saucers, industrial-sized teapots and jugs of milk. Once again, Natalia blessed the English love of tea breaks, and even managed to grab two chocolate biscuits before Mark finished them off.

It was nearly four o'clock by the time they headed downstairs, chatting together and feeling relaxed. Unfortunately the mood was not to last. As they returned to their desks, mayhem broke out.

Avon's wail was so loud this time, Natalia

expected people in Baker Street could hear it. Once again, her distress brought people crowding round her desk. All too soon, the goodwill generated upstairs and at Rasheda's party on Saturday was in danger of completely evaporating.

'I don't believe it,' she cried. 'Look!'

A dustsheet had been laid over her desk. When she lifted it there was a collective intake of breath followed by smothered giggles. The prankster had gone for broke this time.

Lying on the desk was a Frankenstein's Monster, made up of all kinds of lost property. The 'head' was a blonde toupee above spectacles and a false nose and moustache. The torso was a very moth-eaten old jumper, the legs were some very shiny boxer's shorts, and the feet were wellington boots. There were also several sheets of paper bearing the words 'Read My Designer Labels'.

'Not bad, is it life or art, or art is life? Do we care?' Mark drawled, imitating an art critic and posing in front of it, little finger raised. 'Let's call Saatchi and Saatchi, or Tate Modern. We could make a mint out of this if we put it in for the Turner Prize!'

'It's disgusting. I hate it. Why me? Why am I getting all this, all this–' Angrily, Avon grabbed the pieces of paper and screwed them into a ball. 'Rubbish! That's what it is. It's not clever at all.'

'It's not meant to be clever. It's just meant to give us a laugh,' Mark corrected.

'In the bin, that's how I deal with rubbish,' Avon was saying loudly, dusting her hands, ignoring him. 'They are not funny. Donna, I think it's time we started taking fingerprints.'

'Fingerprints – I think we'd better leave that decision to our case sergeant. I suppose we'll have to call him out again.'

'I'll phone the police right away,' Rose said.

'I see. Yes, you'd better,' Donna said reluctantly.

'We need fingerprints – oh, they can dust that paper.' Avon was on her knees now, scrabbling in her waste-paper bin. 'Or ... or test for DNA samples. You can track down anybody these days from just a flake of skin.'

'Calm down, Avon, let's be sensible about this.'

For the first time, Avon rounded on her boss. 'It's all very well saying calm down. You've not been violated like I have.'

'That's putting it a bit strongly.'

'Well, I won't stand for it. I won't. I'm doubling the security guards and you,' she glared at Natalia. 'Isn't it about time you came up with something on the CCTV?'

'Your desk was clear when I came up,' Mark said. 'I was checking the football scores online, like I said.'

'Lie-detector tests. That's what I want.

Everyone in the office to take the test.' Avon looked round her wildly.

'Avon, come into my office and we'll discuss your suggestions calmly.'

Donna's decisive tones halted Avon's hysteria mid flow. Bristling with importance, she tapped after Donna, closing the door behind her unnecessarily loudly.

Natalia returned quietly to her old desk and sat down. Only two people had been missing while they were all upstairs. Cliff. And Stefan. Stefan would have had more than enough time to come down and arrange the hoax on Avon's desk. Avon could easily say that he had left the boardroom at anytime, and who could back him up? Natalia suspected the only reason Avon had not grassed him up so far was because she didn't want to believe it could be him.

As she put her coat on, preparing to go home, Stefan came towards her from the vault.

'Not staying late?'

'Nuala's teacher has asked us to go to her school this evening. We don't know what it's about. We hope she's not in any more trouble. Have you got a date tonight?'

'Not tonight.'

'Stefan–'

'Natalia, I–'

'You first,' she said.

'It wasn't me, I swear to you.'

'What wasn't?'

'The hoax this afternoon. You saw me coming in ... but I did not put out that hoax. I am not the Hoaxer. I can prove it.'

She put a hand on his arm. 'I know you didn't. And Stefan, you're my friend. I didn't suspect you anyway.'

'You didn't?'

'I think you wanted a cigarette. You ran downstairs but it was still raining. So you went to the place you sometimes use, though it's against the rules. The Special Items room, using Cliff's key. Am I right?'

Stefan nodded. 'You knew all the time. I did not want you to think I had the diary and not give it to you.'

'I observed that you only smoke very low-tar cigarettes. The smell only lingers a short while on you, unlike Cliff who is a heavier smoker. When you returned this afternoon I could smell the fresh scent of tobacco on you. I've noticed it before, when you haven't been outside. There's only one place you could go, and you would not have had time to lay out that complicated hoax.'

'That's right. And Cliff was in there with me smoking. When we came out, there were three customers in reception, so he went to help them.

'He was still there when we came down. So Cliff is not the Hoaxer either.'

Now she had cleared Cliff, with Stefan's

201

help, and Mark had already been cleared, while she had been able to account for the others in the office on the CCTV, who the hell could the Hoaxer be?

20

'At least she's passing on her teacher's letters now,' Dermot said, as he and Natalia hurried into Nuala's school.

'Do you know why Miss Ogwala has asked us here yet? Another problem?'

'I damn well hope not. Kathleen's been giving me earache ever since last Friday's debacle. She can't resist a sly dig, that one.'

Natalia diplomatically avoided saying anything about Kathleen. She'd only ever heard her husband's side of that story and, while she didn't doubt his account, she understood that all versions are coloured with some prejudice. As much as she could, she tried to remain neutral around the subject of Kathleen, not wanting to enflame the situation. Although Kathleen didn't always make nonpartisanship easy.

'When's the family conference? Should I be there?'

'If you're not there, I won't be, either. If we're to discuss Nuala and Connor's future, you're part of that, too.'

'Kathleen doesn't realise just how difficult Nuala is finding her having a new partner, does she? I hope she won't think we are ganging up on her.'

'You'd better start looking up your old textbooks on family session skills. You might be needing them,' Dermot said grimly. 'Oh, Jaysus.'

They'd reached Room Eleven and Dermot had looked through the glass window in the door.

'Kathleen's there. I didn't know she was coming, too. I hope we don't need your skills right now.'

'What about Nuala?'

'Can't see her. And no sign of Miss Ogwala yet. We'd better go in.'

'What is she doing here?' were the first words Kathleen hurled across the room. It seemed no matter how non-partisan Natalia wanted to be, Kathleen had drawn enemy lines between them a long time ago.

'I could wait outside, Dermot.'

'No, you're my wife. You're part of this.'

Before matters could get ugly, the door opened behind them and Miss Ogwala came in. 'Good evening, Mr and Mrs O'Shea. Please take a seat.'

They sat in a row in front of Miss Ogwala's desk, rather like three naughty schoolchildren. She wore the same dull maroon suit, the skirt covering her knees, and sensible, lace-up shoes as the other day. The teacher regarded them steadily over half-moon glasses till Natalia began to feel nervous, then finally she spoke.

'Nuala told me she wanted me to lift the ban and allow her back into the Christmas show. I agreed, as long as she apologised to the girl she was bullying. Is this acceptable to you?'

They all nodded. Natalia almost expected her to tell them to speak up.

'She was very specific that she wanted her father and mother to be here to watch, which is why I asked you to come tonight. It will give you an opportunity to view her work in case you have any comments. Is that clear?'

Again, they all nodded.

'Good. She also specified that she did not want her stepfather present—'

'She hasn't got a stepfather—'

'That's Nathan, my new partner.'

'I'd like your views on this,' Miss Ogwala said.

They all looked at one another, then Natalia spoke into the silence. 'She's not quite used to sharing her mother yet. You've not been together long, I think.'

'Two months, sure, but we've been getting on like a house on fire. I'm not convinced it's the right thing to do, to let her have her way in this.'

Miss Ogwala nodded. 'If that's the only problem then I shall leave you to work it out between yourselves. If you'll wait outside for a few moments, I'll then take you to the rehearsals. Nuala has already apologised to the victim of her bullying and undertaken not to do it again. Do you need to see her do it, too?'

'No,' they chorused and stepped into the corridor.

'Why do I feel like I've been told off, now? I didn't think Nathan was such a big deal. She never said anything. He really likes the kids. I left him playing footie with Connor to come down here.'

'Nathan's playing football with Connor tonight?'

'Connor's happy as long as you or Nathan is playing some sort of game with him. You'll have to meet Nathan. We'll all go out for a drink together some time.'

Suddenly, the antagonism of earlier was muted, and Kathleen was all smiles. This was one of Dermot's major complaints about his ex-wife. He could never be sure which mood he would find her in. One day, she was all smiles, planning to order in new curtains; the next day he came home to find his wife and children gone, and a note on the kitchen table saying she had got a job in London and taken the kids with her.

Dermot and Natalia murmured what a

good idea it was, though Natalia saw the flash in Dermot's eye that said, that's not something to look forward to. But she also knew he was intent on continuing to build bridges and repair the damage done by the years apart from his children, and so he would even endure an evening getting to know Kathleen's new love.

Natalia was still surprised that Nuala had changed so rapidly. She'd expected her to hold out much longer. It proved, though, how keen she was to perform in the show. She hoped that, once it was over, this would prove to be a lasting change.

Miss Ogwala joined them and led the trio to the very modern auditorium. There were a handful of people in the audience, and the lights were still up. Children and teachers moved about onstage, in what appeared to Natalia to be a chaotic fashion. Beside her, Dermot and Kathleen were conducting a stilted conversation about Connor and Nuala, and their progress at school. They both seemed to be trying hard not to annoy the other. Then, suddenly, the stage seemed to be ready, and the performance began.

Nuala had waved the script under Natalia's nose at one point, so she knew she appeared about half-way through. As the young cast scrambled about on stage, missing cues and fluffing lines, she began to feel nervous again. This was so important to the young girl's self-esteem. If this went wrong in some way, it could tip her back into her aggressive behaviour again.

Dermot's fingers started to dig into her hand, so fierce was his concentration as they waited for Nuala to appear centre stage. Neither of them had seen her perform before. Would she remember her words and hit all the right notes? Would she keep her word and not lash out in any way at the girl who had been her victim? They had learned she was one of the backing singers.

Then, there she was, stepping confidently towards the microphone. The spotlight wavered the wrong way, then found and followed her, making her dress sparkle. As if she were born to it, she adjusted the microphone, and then launched into her up-tempo song.

'She's a little Kylie,' Dermot breathed, his fingers relaxing slightly.

As Nuala sang and made her moves in time to the music, her eyes sought out her father and mother, Kathleen and Dermot. She was performing just for her mum and dad and loving every minute of it. Natalia let out a long-pent-up breath. The girl showed she had talent and guts to get up and perform, despite everything that had occurred before. That would surely boost her confidence. She just prayed her bullying would become something of the past.

21

'You've been a bit quiet since the rehearsal,' Dermot said. They were lying in bed together, having turned off the light. 'Something bothering you? It's not Nuala, is it? She seemed ... well, less teenagery tonight.'

'She has a lovely voice and real stage presence. You must be very proud of her.'

'I am – wasn't she great? And she didn't even try to upstage the backing girls.'

'It meant everything to her to have you and Kathleen watching her.' She remembered as well, how Nuala had quite spontaneously given her a hug, too, when they'd been congratulating her afterwards.

'I suppose we had to bury the hatchet some time. She's not quite the same selfish, thoughtless woman I got divorced from. Or maybe it's just that I don't have to live with her any more.' He snuggled up close to Natalia. 'Thank God I found you, and you agreed to come and live in London.'

'When I think I am beginning to understand my new country, I find I haven't even started. It's like the shipping news.'

'Are you talking about the novel or the film?'

'No!' she gave him a playful poke in the ribs. 'I mean the weather for ships on the radio. It's for captains of boats, with names of places that nobody knows where they are like Fastnet and Rockall. But the English treasure it, write books about it, and want it never to change. Like the football results.'

'Ah, the footie results. Now you're talking. We must have our Saturday results and the pools coupons.

'Of course they mustn't change,' he continued. 'It's things like the shipping forecast and "Lillibulero", the signature tune to the BBC's World Service, that bind this little nation together. All cosy and safe, an in-joke,' Dermot explained.

'Don't talk to me about in-jokes. I think I'll never understand them.' She turned on her side, curving herself to fit against Dermot's body, and he put his arm around her.

'Not regretting coming here to live, are you? You're worried about something more than BBC radio programmes.'

'I don't regret it for an instant. I love you, Dermot O'Shea, whether you like it or not.'

'I like.'

She sighed. 'It's ... I have to decide something. What the right thing to do is.'

'Is it your hoaxer?'

'No, it's–'

'Don't tell me, it's your missing woman.' Dermot sat up in bed and switched on the bedside light. 'Tell me about it, or we'll never get to sleep.'

Natalia sat up beside him. 'It's Peter Bookman. He told me that he and his wife were having IVF treatment and it put a strain on their marriage. They had a terrible row.'

'And when, pray tell, did you find out all this?'

'Yesterday. At the British Library. He followed me. He thought I'd either kidnapped Helen, drugging her with her own tablets, or that we were in a conspiracy together. Imagine.' Natalia laughed, but it sounded unconvincing even to her ears. 'But he believed me in the end.'

'Bloody hell, Nat. The man was stalking you, and you're telling me this now. Is there anything else you've left out?'

'Well, her shoes were bloodstained. Avon found them. But Peter explained that.'

'Oh, well, if he explained the blood, then it's all OK then.' Dermot's voice rose as he sat up higher in bed. 'Please don't tell me you brought those home with you tonight.'

'No, they're in my drawer at the Lost Property Office. I don't know what to do about them. That's what I'm trying to decide.'

Dermot was silent for a moment, then he said, 'I want you to promise me you'll phone the police station in charge of the Bookman case. Tell them where you work, and that you're the one who found Helen Bookman's

210

belongings and handed them to her husband. Now you've got her shoes, do they want them? OK?'

'I did leave messages, but I didn't want to mention the blood and alarm them. They must have just thought I was wasting their time because they still haven't called back. But now I think you're right. I think that's why I haven't handed them straight over to him. I want Helen to be found safe and well more than anything, whereas at first I wanted to help her husband, too. He said he didn't care what I did with the shoes.'

'Well, if he pulls any more stunts like that you're to phone me, and then the police, in that order. Understand?'

'Yes, boss.' She kissed him lightly on the lips.

'Good. Can we get some sleep now?'

'Yes, boss.'

As she drifted into sleep, Natalia was glad that Dermot hadn't commented on the light bruise on her arm, caused by Peter Bookman's tight fingers. Although she'd tried to make light of the incident, her feelings were still churned up by Peter's behaviour. She was still unable to completely separate out how much of this was because it dredged up painful memories from her own past, or was entirely a response to Peter himself.

Either way, Dermot was right. She'd hand the shoes, everything, over to the police.

22

As Natalia ascended the escalator from the labyrinth of tunnels under Bank underground station, she felt a flutter of excitement. Omar's summons had been so mysterious – what on earth could he want?

'I'd like you to come here to CCTV headquarters,' was all he'd said. 'How soon can you get away?'

It was nearly the end of the day, so Natalia had replied she could be there in half an hour, tubes permitting.

The Bakerloo and Central Lines obliged. The day had been routine until then, giving her the opportunity to make hypotheses, test them out, reject or accept them. She found these fallow periods were often followed by a burst of new ideas. Now, Natalia found time in the cramped carriages to go over the strange twists of the case thus far. When Sherlock Holmes played his violin, however badly, she reckoned he was giving his subconscious a chance to work things out.

The Central Line at Bank was very deep underground and there were several sets of escalators to negotiate on the way out. As she finally emerged into a misty dusk, streetlamps softly glowing through the murk of a London evening, she fought against the tide of suited bankers on their way home for the day. Taxis zipped up and down Threadneedle Street, and Natalia made her way past the neo-Classical façade of the Bank of England. So evocative, these English names: Cornhill, Poultry, so redolent of history. The Bank of Poland too was steeped in history – a short and tragic one – having been rebuilt after the destruction wreaked in the Second World War.

Natalia's mobile rang and she moved to the convenient shelter of a Costa coffee shop and, finger pressed against her free ear to hear better, answered it.

'Detective Sergeant Alison Kane. You left some messages for me to call you.'

There was a note of impatience in the way the policewoman spoke, but Natalia chose to ignore it, and put on her best friendly voice. 'Yes, thank you for calling back. It's about the Bookman case. Helen Bookman, the missing woman.'

'Yes, I know the case,' DS Kane said, 'and I'm not at liberty to discuss it with unconnected members of the general public.'

'But I work for the Lost Property Office–' said Natalia.

'I'm not sure Mrs Bookman constitutes lost property, Miss–'

'O'Shea.'

'Miss O'Shea. So unless you have any fresh information–'

'Well, that's exactly it,' said Natalia, feeling herself approach dangerously close to her anger threshold, 'if you'd let me finish.' DS Kane was silent. 'I work for the Lost Property Office, and I wanted to help Mr Bookman after seeing his posters. I found his missing wife's scarf and handbag. He told you?'

Natalia thought she could hear the rattle of a keyboard in the background. 'Right. Peter's also given us the copy of your CCTV tape, too. Say again about Helen's possessions.'

The policewoman's tone had lost its smug superiority, and Natalia felt a glow of pride at having cracked that tough exterior. A man exiting the coffee shop gave Natalia a friendly, but shyly appreciative glance as he walked past, and she did her best to show him the wedding band on her left hand while explaining her findings to DS Kane.

'Our records showed that her scarf, handbag and shoes were found together on the Circle Line on the Friday she went missing.' Thirteen days ago, she realised, with a shiver.

'Handed in at High Street Ken, right?'

'Yes. And then we saw CCTV footage showing her leaving the items on purpose. It

214

wasn't a case of forgetting.'

'I've reviewed the CCTV footage,' was DS Kane's unhelpful response. 'Do you have anything new to tell me?'

'Yes,' said Natalia. 'The shoes were missing, but now I've found them.' She paused. 'They have bloodstains on them.'

'I see. Where are they now?'

'At the LPO.'

'I'll arrange for someone to collect them.' Natalia could hear the unmistakeable sounds of the other woman already shifting papers on her desk, eager to get onto her next job. But she wasn't going to let her go yet, despite the traffic noises around her. She knew how she must sound to the detective – like just another nosey member of the public, but perhaps she was in a privileged position: There was something Peter Bookman was lying about, hiding from both the police and her. Natalia had no doubt it was linked to his wife's disappearance.

'I've told Mr Bookman. He... Yesterday, I told him. He seemed to think I might be involved, that I am helping his wife, and that's how I found her belongings. He eventually accepted the truth, that I'm not, but my husband thought you should know.' As she spoke, Natalia felt she was betraying Peter's trust, but what choice did he give her, with his odd behaviour.

'Right. And are you?'

'No, not at all! I've never met her.' What else could she say? *I feel I owe it to this woman whom I know only through her picture on a poster.*

'OK. Look, if you're at all worried or feel unsafe, ring me.' She gave her direct line, but to Natalia it sounded as if she were going through the motions.

'Thank you. Do you think Helen will be found? I worry about her. These anti-depressants she's on, might make her behave strangely, yes? Her mother is very worried.'

DS Kane's voice turned cold again. 'You know about her tablets?'

'Peter Bookman told me, yes. He told his mother-in-law that Helen had got a repeat prescription.'

'Miss O'Shea, if you don't mind me saying, you seem to know an awful lot about this case.'

'I'm only trying to help.'

'Can I suggest that you leave that to the professionals. I assure you we're doing everything in our power to...' Natalia began to drift away – she recognised the corporate banalities that people like Avon and Donna were used to trotting out to keep normal people satisfied. '...to a satisfactory con-clusion...'

Her eye was caught by the advertising board for the *Evening Standard* that rested on the pavement beside a portable news-stand. The headline read: *Woman's Body Found in the Thames.*

'Wait,' said Natalia. 'A woman has been found in the river...'

DS Kane sighed heavily. 'Have you any idea, Miss O'Shea, how many bodies we find in the river each year – and that's probably only a fraction of those which float out to sea...'

'But it could be Helen.'

'Enough, Miss O'Shea. I'm going to end this call. Please try to forget about the case and get back to your job.'

Natalia was getting nowhere. 'Perhaps you're–'

The line went dead.

Natalia looked at the display in disbelief. How could anyone be so rude and, well ... so wilfully obtuse? She scurried out of the shop doorway and bought a newspaper from the stallholder, a short, sturdy-looking man who might have been Cliff's brother, but without the beard.

The article began under the picture of a white tent by what looked like a disused warehouse. A diver was half out of the water.

Police are appealing to help from the general public this evening after the body of an un-identified woman was fished out of the River Thames by marine officers. At this time, the police aren't sure whether foul play was involved in the death, and are releasing few details until preliminary examinations have been carried out. They have specified that the victim appears to be between 30 and 50 years old, and that there are no signs of external trauma indicative of an assault. Members of the public are asked to contact the Metropolitan Police on the number below if they have any further information. More details follow on page 2.

Natalia turned over the page, and continued to read.

The officer in charge of the case, Detective Bullmer, briefed the press just after ten o'clock this morning. He told attending journalists: 'We responded to calls from a jogger in the early hours of this morning, and recovered the body of a white female from the river near Wapping. At the moment, we're keeping an open mind as to the cause of death.'

Natalia scanned the rest of the article, reading each word for possible clues that the woman might be Helen Bookman. All details were frustratingly vague, not enough to confirm that the woman matched Helen's description, but at the same time not enough to discount the possibility.

If Helen had run out of her pills, could she have taken her own life? But another thought was the proximity of Wapping to Canary Wharf, where Peter Bookman's office was situated.

Natalia tucked the newspaper under her arm, and waited for a gap in the traffic, then stepped across the road. Omar would be waiting for her, and she prayed he held the answers to her questions.

The great concrete block of CCTV head-quarters reared up before her, like one of the faceless Communist administrative centres Natalia remembered from her youth. Once through the revolving glass doors, Natalia's bag was checked at a metal detector and a security guard gave a quick airport frisk. At last, armed with her visitor's pass, she was permitted entry and met Omar on the other side.

She was surprised by the change in him. Gone was the dour and suspicious expression. Omar flashed a wide smile and clasped her hand warmly, his eyes bright and alive.

'Come with me,' he said, escorting her into a lift. 'I would like you to see what a *real* CCTV room looks like, and then I have something special to show you.'

Natalia fought the urge to ask him to come straight out with what he'd discovered. It seemed somehow rude to impose upon his studied politeness. The lift descended two floors and the doors slid open, revealing a room completely unlike the dusty basement of the LPO. Omar gave a shallow bow and gave a dramatic sweep of his hand.

Bank after bank of screens filled the room, many stations with their own operatives wearing mounted ear and mouthpieces. A low hum of computers filled the air. Two giant plasma screens were mounted on the far wall: one showed some sort of gathering in Trafalgar Square, the other built-up traffic on a shopper-crowded street. There was little chatter, and the clean lines and serenity of the room was a welcome contrast with the bustling, fume-filled streets above.

'This is just one of many rooms we have here,' Omar told her, with relish. 'I'll give you a tour later, but there's something you must see first.'

'This ... this is like Dr Who. Or Houston Command Centre when the space shuttle takes off.'

Omar smiled.

'There are 30,000 CCTV cameras in London,' he said. 'And they all feed into our operations here.'

'Imagine, all those hours and hours of watching to be done. And what are the two big screens for?'

'Our staff can choose to display incidents that they think need special attention.'

Natalia watched in awe as the images changed on the giant screens. Above the room was a glassed-in office looking over the entire area. Inside, she could see men and women looking down while talking on phones or into microphones.

'What's going on up there?'

'They're part of the communications system with the police – our interface, if you like. We report anything we think they should act on, either by radio link, or we can send information direct into the onboard computers in rapid-response vehicles and other police cars.'

'I had no idea all this was going on. Who decides what to pass on, what to advise?'

Omar gave her a sideways look. 'The team up there. Gold Command. That's where I used to be.' His face took on a wistful expression.

'You will be there again,' said Natalia, placing her hand on his arm.

'Perhaps,' said Omar, 'but after the bombings, I am not considered such a friendly face.'

Natalia didn't know what answer to give her new friend, but thankfully he changed the subject first.

'Anyway, I have your hoaxer to track down now, don't I?' He smiled conspiratorially, and Natalia felt her heart drop. So this wasn't about Helen after all.

There was a sudden buzz and the images on the giant screens jumped and changed again, this time to a mass of struggling people that surged forward into an underground station. As those in front stopped, so those behind began to push and apply pressure.

'Football crowds. We'll need to operate a station shutdown before it gets worse and people get injured.' He moved away and spoke into a microphone. Natalia saw the people in the overhanging office galvanised into action, and then Omar was back.

'But this is what I wanted to show you. Come over here, to my terminal.' He led her to a desk a little apart from the others, and tapped at the keyboard. 'I stayed after hours last night, looking for your missing woman. At about ten o'clock I found her!'

So it *was* to do with Helen.

'Well done, Omar! Where?' She was dreading hearing some tube station in East London, anywhere in the vicinity of Wapping.

'Wembley Park.' Natalia felt relief surge through her. It didn't mean anything for certain, of course, but it put the breadth of London between Helen and the place where the body was found. Wembley was miles from the river.

Omar continued, 'You want to know how I found her, yes? Well, she was holding the same carrier bag, and wore the trainers she'd put on, but as you'll see, she'd put her hair up in a ponytail, which is perhaps why you missed her. Look, there.' He froze the tape.

The screen showed passengers alighting from a tube train. One of them was a woman.

Omar had stopped the tape as she looked ahead along the platform, and Natalia was able to get a clear picture of her. It was un-mistakeably Helen Bookman. Natalia felt she'd recognise the face anywhere, which now even haunted her dreams.

'I can't believe it!'

'She's getting off a Jubilee Line train,' said Omar. He let the tape run forward again. They watched as Helen walked slowly up the platform, letting her head drop, letting herself be bumped into by others, uncaring.

'She must have changed from the Circle to the Jubilee at Baker Street. Could she be heading for the Metropolitan now? Let's hope so. If she leaves the station she'll be harder to track.' Natalia spoke with the knowledge born of her recent days as a CCTV operative.

'That's what I'll be looking for next. And if she did take the Metropolitan, she could be on one of three lines, terminating Chesham, Watford or Amersham.'

'Those are a long way beyond north-west London.'

'Yes, in the Home Counties, almost in the countryside. But I will locate her, I'm sure,' Omar said.

'If you stay late again, I will not be Jamila's favourite person.'

'She was understanding yesterday.'

'Good. By the way, what time is Helen

changing trains here?'

'Afternoon of the Friday she went missing.'

'How did you manage it? It must have taken for ever.'

'A process of elimination really,' Omar shrugged, but Natalia could read the secret pride in his eyes. 'I knew the scarf was handed in at Stanmore at the end of the Jubilee Line at an approximate time, so I figured she must have disembarked from that line at some point, so I checked back from there.'

His tone was nonchalant but Natalia imagined it must have taken him the better part of a day poring over surveillance footage.

'OK. I can't thank you enough, Omar. I really think we're getting closer to finding what happened to her.'

'No problem. Anyway, I feel *I* should be thanking *you*.'

'What for?'

'Your dedication to the search for Helen Bookman inspired me. I realised I'd stopped caring some time ago. Instead of making life easier, though, it was not only ruining my reputation but was taking away my self respect.'

Natalia shook her head. 'You found your way again, that's what happened.'

'We won't argue about it,' he smiled

warmly. 'But because of that, it's confirmed I won't be returned to the LPO and it's been decided higher up to close the basement and focus our resources here. You've shown a real aptitude for the work. If you wanted to put in for a transfer and work here, I'd sponsor you. There might even be a pay rise in it.'

'Omar, I don't know what to say. I've enjoyed working with you. Can I think about it? Talk it over with Dermot?'

'Of course.' As they talked, they'd made their way into the lift and were now emerging into reception. Immediately, Natalia's mobile rang before they could say goodbye. She moved to one side to answer it, while Omar went to speak to the security guards. The screen flashed with a withheld number.

'Hello, Natalia here,' she said.

'What the hell have you been telling the police about my wife?' Peter Bookman yelled.

23

'Peter? Mr Bookman? I'm at work. What is it, is there news of Helen?'

'No, there damned well isn't. The police have just rung *me*. What the hell have you been saying to them?' His voice was so loud that Natalia had to hold the phone away from her. She grimaced at Omar.

'I told Detective Sergeant Kane everything that has happened, everything you know already.'

'You must have said something. They've just been here. Showed me a picture of some dead woman. A bloody corpse.'

Natalia held her breath for a few seconds.

'It wasn't Helen?'

'No,' said Peter. 'It was ... hard to tell. They're talking as though Helen might be dead. That policewoman just gave me the third degree again. Haven't I been put through enough?'

'I only confirmed the information about the scarf and bag, what we saw on the CCTV tape–'

'I'm sick of these accusations. They should be out there searching for Helen, I should be on TV begging people to find her. I'm sick of it, do you hear?'

'I hear you, Peter.' Her old training kicked in. Years of listening to distressed parents and troubled youngsters. 'You are angry.'

'Damned right I'm angry. The last thing I need is interfering people like you stirring up rumours against me to the police.'

'Is it the shoes, Peter? Is that what's bothering you?' Natalia was aware of Omar's concerned face watching her.

There was a moment's silence. 'You told

them about the shoes?'

'I did. They're sending someone to the LPO to collect them.'

'Don't you realise what you've done? Sent them off on a wild goose chase after the shoes, instead of doing what's important. I told you what happened. She cut her foot on some glass, for Christ's sake!'

'Peter, please calm down – I felt I had to help the police in any way I could.'

'Help yourself, more like. You just want your minute in the limelight.'

Natalia bit back the reflex to snap back. 'Peter, we have found Helen on the CCTV cameras, the evening she disappeared, at Wembley Park.'

'Really? You're not lying just to–'

'It's true,' Natalia reassured him.

Peter sounded stunned. 'I can't believe it. What on earth was she doing up there?'

'I was hoping you might be able to answer that question,' said Natalia.

'I need time to think,' said Peter. The anger had seeped out of his voice, leaving only a husk of anxiety.

'Think positively, Peter, and keep talking to your friends and family.'

'I will,' he said. 'Goodbye, Natalia.'

'Good–' Peter Bookman hung up on her.

'That sounded difficult,' Omar said, rejoining her side.

'I'm sorry I took that call, but as you could

tell, he was in a state. He had to look at a body. It wasn't Helen, but it must be preying on his mind. He could hardly believe you've traced Helen further.'

As she left Omar for the evening, and went out into the busy streets again, past the pubs and bars filled with noise, light and muted music, Natalia tried to forget the mania in Peter Bookman's voice, his childlike switches from anger to remorse. The body in the water was not Helen Bookman, and for that small mercy she could be grateful. But had Peter's temper flared because he desperately wanted her found – or was he terrified of her being discovered?

Natalia climbed the stairs to her flat, wincing slightly as her new shoes pinched the big toe of her left foot. *I hope they'll wear in*, she thought, and realised the statement could apply not just to leather, but also to her relationship with Nuala. Perhaps eventually they'd wear each other down to a comfortable friendship.

Their apartment block had a controlled entranceway and Natalia and Dermot had their own security code that they had to punch in. The stairway was well maintained, painted white with composition flooring. It was not overly welcoming or stylish, but it was clean and safe.

On the second-floor landing, she got out

her key then stood for a moment, key poised over the lock. She could hear faint sounds of music coming from the other flat on their landing. A young couple lived there, originally from Sri Lanka. The wife was pregnant. Natalia shook her head. She hoped they'd be able to cope with carrying a pushchair up and down the stairs all the time.

Fortunately, the flats were well insulated against noise. She hadn't worried that Nuala's sulks and door slamming the other night would have disturbed the neighbours.

She turned the key, let herself in and put the post she'd carried up from their box by the door on the chair in their little vestibule. Then she took off her coat, hung it up and listened for a moment. Silence. It was still a luxury to her. After growing up in such a big noisy family, with aunts and uncles coming and going all the time, it still felt strange to be by herself for an evening, a rare event in itself.

Dermot was out with Connor, at a fathers-and-sons five-a-side football match at the nearby sports centre. It was not her night to have the kids, but Kathleen had arranged to spend an evening together with Nuala, just the two of them. The kind of evening Nuala had been missing since Nathan had arrived on the scene. It was good for Dermot and Connor to spend time together, too – she wasn't sure which of the two boys were more excited at the prospect.

Natalia had already planned her evening. She'd have some soup and fruit, followed by a naughty chocolate sponge pudding. Then she'd have a long, hot soak in the bath, and after that she'd settle on the settee with her laptop and catch up on e-mails with her mum, and her friend Marta, who'd promised to send photos of the little girl she and her husband had recently adopted.

Her sore toe forgotten, she picked up the bundle of envelopes and made her way to the kitchen. She was going to switch the kettle on when she changed her mind and reached instead inside the fridge and poured herself a glass of white wine from the open bottle in there.

She took the red rubber band from around the post and cast a glance through it. As expected, a couple of early Christmas cards, some junk mail, a bill, and then ... she stiffened. The long oblong envelope bore an airmail sticker and Turkish stamps. She knew the handwriting from long familiarity. It was from her former sister-in-law in Antalya.

But the letter was early. Her annual photo of her dear Paul usually arrived on Christmas Eve, a kind touch that Natalia appreciated. Her heart quickened. Could something be wrong?

Natalia stared at the envelope again, before picking it up and tearing it open. She felt perspiration break out on her forehead and her stomach threatened to knot. A photograph fell out, wrapped in a sheet of folded paper, with nothing written on it, as per usual. Her hand flew to the photograph and she turned it over.

'Oh, you handsome boy,' she murmured, tears immediately tickling her lower lashes as she stared hungrily at the photo, taking in every detail. Paul was wearing a football strip, Manchester United colours she guessed, and was standing in a garden, squinting into the sun and grinning cheerily. His bushy eyebrows and heavy lashes, both courtesy of his father's genes, softened the angle in his face. A front tooth was missing.

'My, but you've grown in the past year,' she said, and then, as always, the sorrow gripped her. She willed herself not to weep but a single tear threaded down her cheek

She remembered the last time she ever saw Paul. She'd taken her son to kindergarten, as always, on her way to work. They had a special crèche that opened early for working mothers. Her own mother had offered to look after him and take him later, but she'd wanted to keep as much as possible to their normal routine. He'd been wearing a pair of blue jeans and a dark-blue T-shirt top with his favourite dinosaur sticker on the front.

She'd kissed him and he'd run happily into the playroom. 'Bye bye, Mama,' were the last words she'd heard him say.

Natalia had been with a client when the news came. It was her mother who phoned.

'My darling,' she said, and there was something in her tone that set her senses to full alert.

'What is it? Is it Grandpa?' He'd had a bad chest infection and they'd been worried about pneumonia setting in.

'No it's ... it's Paul.'

Natalia could not stop the involuntary moan that had escaped her lips. Her mother's instincts were all powerful.

'My baby – is he hurt?'

'No, at least we think he's all right. I'm sure he is–'

'Tell me!' She tried not to shriek.

'It's Jem. He's taken Paul.'

She was filled with fury, but also a strange relief. Fury because she had offered Jem every opportunity to discuss shared parenting through an intermediary, but he'd refused to even answer. Intense relief because Paul was not ill, or injured in any way. At first she'd felt it would simply be a matter of time before she and her son were reunited. But as the conversation went on, the feeling of dread welled up within her, making her legs heavy and her heart pound faster.

She learned that Jem had arrived at the

kindergarten during playtime. He'd been friendly and polite and the inexperienced minder had been put off-guard, although they knew that Natalia and Jem had split up, and he had not arranged to see his little boy. He said he'd brought Paul's favourite toy that he'd left behind. Paul, of course, was overjoyed to see his daddy and had hurled himself into his arms. Jem had scooped him up and hugged him. It was at that moment a scuffle had broken out among the other children.

'I only looked away for a few seconds. When I turned round he was through the gate,' the teacher explained, very distressed. 'I ran after him but the car was waiting with the door open, engine running, and they drove off very fast.'

That would have been one of Jem's friends helping him, Natalia was sure.

She had hardly slept for the next week, always hearing Paul crying out to her. She saw him everywhere. If she did sleep, in her dreams she was always looking for him, catching glimpses as he disappeared round corners, or up escalators. She thought she would not be able to survive the loss but somehow, with the support of her family, she did.

She threw herself into the search for Paul, but the snatch had been well planned. She'd expected nothing less from Jem They'd driven to the border and got out of Poland that way, most likely. They weren't recorded on a boat or a plane.

The next year was shrouded in darkness. Natalia barely remembered any of it. She'd hauled herself through the daily round, despite the sense of pointlessness. And then the first photo had arrived. At least she knew he was safe and well. Some healing could begin, but the wound would never close over, not until she saw him once more. But the pictures gave her a spark of hope, and she went to the desk, unlocked the bottom drawer and pulled out the file to place the most recent one with the others – her only true son, growing up in two dimensions.

She was thankful Dermot was not there to witness her display of emotions. He suffered for her and would start making unrealistic suggestions about going to Turkey and 'finding that bastard and planting one on him'.

Thank you, Fatima, she thought to herself, and picked up the envelope to throw it in the bin. And then she noticed it. On the back flap of the envelope Fatima had written her return address. She could hardly believe it. Tears welled up again, but this time they were tears of joy. Now, she could write back, make contact.

Now anything was possible.

24

Passing the statue of Sherlock Holmes on her way into work the next morning, Natalia was ninety-nine per cent convinced as to the identity of the Hoaxer. Fatima's letter, and the beacon of hope it represented, had ensured a peaceful night's rest, and as she walked the remaining distance to the office, the pieces clicked into place.

Indeed, Mr Watson. Wanting to look at the Internet as soon as possible, she hurried straight to her computer terminal on entering the office.

'What's up, Nat?' Mark called out. 'You look like the cat who's got the cream. Where'd you slope off to last night?'

'And there was me trying to be so careful,' she laughed. 'You spotted me!'

'Now you're being all mysterious. Admit it, you were off to buy me a Christmas present, weren't you?'

Cheeky Mark. No, you're not the Hoaxer. He'd been checking out the fantasy football leagues, a trail of dates and times that could be easily double-checked on the computers.

She typed 'Sherlock Holmes famous sayings' into Google.

Stefan swanned through the office, humming to himself and drawing in his wake the waves of some expensive fragrance.

'Going for a cigarette already Stefan?'

Stefan gazed at her serenely with his dark, navy eyes. 'Is sunny today. Lovely fresh air out there – cough, cough.'

Natalia clicked on the first search result.

Neither was Stefan the Hoaxer. He was her friend, and she trusted him. He'd been smoking in the Special Items room at key moments – he and Cliff. They were both in the clear. She watched as Stefan nodded to Rose as he passed. Rose had been on holiday while several hoaxes took place. She was the only member of staff close enough to senior-level management to gain as to the keys.

And there it was, the great Arthur Conan Doyle, in the guise of his greatest creation:

'When you have eliminated the impossible, whatever remains, *however improbable*, must be the truth?'

Natalia carefully considered Avon, who was tapping her watch meaningfully as Ranjiv sidled in late. She had thought for some time that Avon herself might be the culprit. She fitted the profile of a shoe and bag lover, and would undertake deviousness to get her bands on objects she desired, but theft? Humiliation? No, that was not Avon's style. And she had been in full view all the

time the Frankenstein Monster was ass-
embled. Avon was not someone you could
miss.

The *motive* behind the hoaxes, that was
the issue that had eluded her. Understand
the motive, and one understands the
culprit. And that guidance had come from a
source she never would have expected: Peter
Bookman. As she had considered their
fraught conversation while soaking in the
bath, one phrase had repeatedly jarred.

You just want your minute in the limelight.

Now Natalia knew enough of herself to
realise that was completely untrue, but it
was interesting that Peter should see her
interest as attention seeking, after all she'd
done to help.

She glanced again at her colleagues
around the office. Ranjiv, Poppy, Jim – not
only would they have found it difficult to
gain access to the keys, they never had any
real call to go into the vault, so their presence would have been commented on.
That, combined with the fact they never left
the meeting room once during the team-
building exercise, eliminated them as suspects. Which left only one member of staff –
however improbable that supposition was.

Natalia tapped on Donna's door, and went
in. 'I'd like to talk with you. Is now a convenient time?' she asked.

237

'Sure, that's what I'm here for, Natalia. Sit down, please.'

'Thanks.' Natalia sat in what was usually Avon's chair. Donna wore a black suit with a red top, and had twisted her hair up into a knot and secured it with two Chinese pins. Self consciously, Natalia flicked back her own straight, unstyled hair.

'What's the problem then?'

'Not a problem, exactly. I wanted to talk about–'

Donna's mobile rang. She picked it up and looked at the caller display. 'Got to take this. Excuse me, it'll only take a minute.'

Natalia made to stand up but Donna waved her back down. Trying not to eavesdrop on what was clearly a breezy, almost flirtatious, conversation, she let her eyes wander round the office Donna's coat hung neatly on a hanger on the aluminium and Perspex hat stand. The fiery bird-of-paradise plant was as healthy and vigorous as its owner But her eyes finally came to rest on Donna's cupboard She fingered the object in her pocket, the reason she'd risen early and visited Rasheda on the way to work that morning.

She flicked her gaze to Donna, and saw that she was watching her closely. 'OK, Phil, I have to go, one of my staff is waiting. I'll call you back on that.' She put down her phone, and placed both palms on the desk.

'I'm sorry, Natalia, what was it you wanted to speak with me about?'

Natalia took a deep breath. 'The Hoaxer.'

Donna's smiled raised a millimetre and, if Natalia hadn't been on her guard, or if it had been another day, she wouldn't have noticed it.

'Ah, yes, it's been a nuisance. Do you have any new information?'

'I think I know who it is,' said Natalia.

Donna's eyes left hers as she peered over her head into the office behind. 'Well, don't keep me in suspenders. Pray tell.' Her voice had taken on a brisk camaraderie.

'I think it was you, Donna.'

After a brief pause, Donna let out a high-pitched whinny and sat back in her chair.

'Me? I've never heard anything so preposterous. What would I gain from those silly posters?'

The fact that she hadn't denied it gave Natalia the confidence to go on. 'I asked myself the same question,' she said, looking into her lap. 'I thought it might be to keep us all on our toes, to help make the office run smoothly, but then I realised it's much more personal than that. I don't really want to say...'

'You had *better* say,' said Donna. 'You've made a serious, and *personal*, accusation.'

Hearing Donna's suddenly fierce tone, and pinned by the dagger look in her eye,

Natalia felt her first niggle of doubt.

'Would you mind opening that cupboard,' she said, pointing to the side of Donna's chair.

The spell was broken, and Donna stared at the cupboard, presumably weighing up her options. This was make or break time, Natalia realised.

'I ... I'm afraid I don't have the key,' said Donna.

Natalia pulled out Rasheda's spare from her pocket. 'I do.'

Donna's face drained of colour. 'Where did you get that?'

Natalia didn't answer the question. She didn't want to get her friend involved. She merely nodded at the cupboard. 'Can I?'

Donna raised her chin defiantly. 'You *may* not,' she said.

The door behind opened and Avon stuck her head through the door. Her eyes were furtive as a ferret's.

'I heard raised voices – is everything all right?'

Natalia turned back to Donna, who met her eyes, and sensed defeat.

'No, Avon, everything's quite all right. Please leave us alone.'

With disappointment etched in her face, Avon retreated.

After the door clicked closed, Donna spoke. 'How did you know, Natalia?'

'A process of elimination,' she replied, consciously echoing Omar's words. 'You were the only member of staff I couldn't account for. You were the only one – other than Stefan, whose whereabouts *have* been accounted for – who slipped out. It was when you said you went to arrange the sandwiches. Then I saw you speaking with Chief Inspector Crane from the Transport Police. I should have made the final connection yesterday – it was your reluctance.'

'My what?'

'On Tuesday, when Rose said she would call the police about the hoax, you were reluctant for her to place the call. Why? I remembered Avon telling me there is a policeman you find sexy. And we all noticed that on some days you wear a short skirt and make-up, with your hair down.'

'I didn't realise I was being observed so minutely.'

'Those were the hoax days, I realised – every hoax meant you had to call in the policeman and gave you a chance to meet him. Which means you always knew in advance when he was coming.'

Donna chuckled ruefully. 'God you make me sound like a sad old spinster.' Her eyes briefly met Natalia's, and they were full of sadness. 'I suppose I am, in a way.'

'No, you're not–'

'You're right – I guess I am a bit obsessed

with the guy. He's gorgeous, isn't he? I wasn't planning on continuing the hoaxes forever, just until I got to know him better. Then I would have stopped. I thought a few light-hearted hoaxes would be laughed off as pranks, not hurt anyone.'

'You don't have to explain yourself to me,' said Natalia. 'But what about poor Avon?'

Donna looked a bit uncomfortable. 'Well, no one was injured. I think everyone saw the joke. Found it a laugh.'

'Except for Avon, your target. She admires you.'

'I didn't exactly target her. Her desk just happened to be nearest. As my second-in-command, I expect most from her. I'm sure she'll understand.'

Natalia imagined Avon struggling with the truth, and finally allowing Donna's smooth spin to win her round. But the deception would still rankle, deep inside.

'I directed quite a few at myself,' said Donna. 'I thought Avon could handle it though, especially if I reassured her in private not to worry about the posters. Anyway, I think some of the other personnel quite enjoyed it, don't you?' She gave Natalia a little smile.

'I'm not interested in hoaxes so much,' said Natalia, 'but I think you have something in your cupboard that I've been looking for.'

Turning in her seat, Donna took her key ring and opened the lock. Natalia stood up and came to her side. As the cupboard door swung open, she stared at the contents.

Most prominent were the Impala horns. There were dentures, a wig, a very large bra, the top half of a wet suit, a prosthetic limb, a brightly coloured plastic toy, and other things buried underneath. A digital camera for taking the pictures.

And a diary. The initials HB were inscribed on the front.

'Helen's diary!'

She reached in and took it, holding it firmly in both hands. She rubbed her fingers gently over the gilt letters, and the clasp, as if to make sure it was real.

'Is it special?' said Donna. 'The owner was unidentifiable, that's why I had it here. If anyone had come to collect it, of course I'd have handed it over.'

Donna surely had absolutely no idea of what she'd done. She would not have connected the name on the poster, which was still pinned up on the office notice-board, with the initials on the diary – even if she had really noticed the initial themselves.

'You see the initials? HB is for Helen Bookman. The missing woman on the poster I put up.'

Donna stared at her, slight colour staining her neck. 'I had no idea.'

'There may be vital information in here for the police and her husband. About where she was going, who she was meeting, her state of mind.'

'I really had no idea,' Donna apologised.

'The important thing is that I can now return it to Helen's husband.'

'I haven't read it,' said Donna. 'I wouldn't dream of doing that.'

'Of course not,' said Natalia, and she could tell that her boss was telling the truth. Whatever her misguided actions, she was essentially a good person.

Natalia made for the door, but Donna jumped up and put a hand on her arm. 'Natalia, maybe it would be better if we kept this between the two of us. I promise my days as the Hoaxer are over.'

Natalia was never the sort to seek out a position of power, and now she found herself wielding it, the feeling was uncomfortable. She'd thought only as far as confronting the culprit, never exposure.

'There must be something I can do?' said Donna, mistaking her hesitation for a bargaining tactic.

Inspiration seized Natalia, and she began talking in Donna's language. 'How about,' she suggested, 'setting up some kind of drive – shoes for homeless people. The people who live on the streets of London.' A vision came to her of Homeless Joe in a smart pair of city

244

brogues. She smiled. 'We sell off unclaimed items after three months for charity. Why not donate the suitable shoes? How's that for a deal?'

'Excellent idea. Gets publicity, reflects well on this department. The guys upstairs will like it. I'll get onto it right away.' They both stood up and Donna held out her hand stiffly. 'No more hoaxes, I promise. I'm sure I'll hook Phil another way one of these days – maybe I could persuade him to be my Marathon training buddy!'

This woman would always find an angle, Natalia thought. 'I must go, deliver the diary,' she said, taking Donna's hand.

In a matter of a few minutes, Natalia found herself on the street, warmly wrapped up in coat, scarf and gloves against the cold of the first day of December. Overhead was a leaden grey sky, and shoppers and tourists alike scurried along, heads bent. She halted. What should her next course of action be? She had felt such urgency to get on the move with the diary, she had not thought what she should do next.

Dermot had asked her to call him if anything developed.

Detective Sergeant Alison Kane had given Natalia her private number. She ought to call and arrange to take the diary to her. On the other hand, her first commitment had been to Peter Bookman; it was only when doubt began to set in that her allegiance to Helen had deepened.

The diary was almost burning a hole in her hand. It might hold nothing more than dates and times and places. Or it might contain more of Helen's thoughts and feelings. How she longed to find out more about her. It would be wrong to pry into Helen's private world, but what alternative did she have?

Helen, what shall I do to find you?

She tried to listen, to hear Helen's voice. She closed her eyes for a second. What had brought her to this moment? It was Helen herself, that look in her eyes that had called to Natalia and found an answering echo.

Helen, we've never met, but I hope we will, and you will understand and forgive me for what I am about to do. But time is running out fast. There is no other way. She unclasped and opened up the diary. Quickly, she flicked through the gold-edged leaves to November, to the middle of November, to Friday two weeks ago.

There, in the middle of the page, in Helen's bold and clear black pen, was a note of an appointment.

'TP, lunchtime, Canary Wharf.'

TP? Who could that be? It took Natalia less than ten minutes to find out.

25

'Come up. Third floor.' Peter Bookman's voice echoed tinnily through the intercom. The door release buzzed and Natalia pushed her way in. The lobby was ultra modern, a new development of apartments in St John's Wood, it was painted off-white with a dark, marble floor.

Crossing over to the lifts, Natalia pictured Helen doing the same the day she went missing, the day she'd gone to Canary Wharf to meet 'TP' for lunch. So at least that explained why she'd taken trainers with her that day.

As she rode the lift to the third floor, her throat went dry from nerves and she found it hard to breathe. She could hear Dermot scolding her. 'Didn't I tell you not to go near that man on your own?' *I left you a message*, she told him silently. His phone had been switched off, which probably meant he was engaged in a dangerous manoeuvre involving heavy machinery. She'd also left a message at the police station making both calls from the back of a black cab, but knowing how long it had taken the police to return her calls in the past, she didn't hold much hope of them swooping in if things should turn ugly.

She'd phoned Peter's mobile earlier, only to find it switched off, and his home number was on answer phone, so she'd hung up and tried his office. When the receptionist told her he was not in today, she'd asked for his address, only to be put through to one of his colleagues who with much reluctance finally gave out his address.

Peter was at the door of his flat, beckoning to her. He wore a pair of washed-out blue jeans and a sweatshirt inside out. His feet were bare. It seemed that as Helen had disappeared, so had the smart-suited businessman Natalia first met. He closed the front door, led her across a corridor, and into a large room, which was in semi-darkness. 'I couldn't face the office today,' he said, his voice low and lifeless. 'I felt, what's the point? Money, work – nothing matters any more, does it?'

Natalia noticed that he was staring fixedly at her handbag, as if willing his eyes to bore a hole into it. Immediately, he demanded to see Helen's diary. But first she insisted he open the Roman blinds.

Peter did as bidden and wintry light illuminated the dust on the glass coffee table. Natalia was standing in a large, open-plan living space. The floor was carpeted in a neutral pale sand, enlivened with bright rugs.

The walls were painted a pale-rose colour, and were dominated by two very large modern abstracts. She wondered if they were original Rothkos, or prints. Nearest the window and facing it, was a black-leather settee and two matching armchairs arranged around the coffee table. There was room for a table and chairs and beyond was a breakfast bar and kitchen. Presumably the bathroom and bedroom led off from the corridor by the front door. But what struck Natalia most was the slovenliness.

Dirty plates were stacked on most of the available spaces in the open-plan kitchen and the breakfast bar that separated it from the living area. A vase of dried-out and drooping lilies needed cleaning out, and the whole place smelt stale. Peter seemed to have completely given up, his stubble bristling along his jawline, and his eyes deep set and without lustre. Catching sight of an empty brandy bottle, Natalia wondered whether he'd been sleeping downstairs to avoid his vacant marital bed.

The settee and chairs had bright cushions, and from where she stood Natalia could see jolly Mediterranean-style pottery in the kitchen, and here and there in both rooms, in a variety of forms and media, were little pigs. Helen's touch, surely, which broke up the formality of the living space.

'Do you want to sit down?' Peter gestured,

his fingers twitching spasmodically.

Natalia sat and he came and sat beside her on the leather settee. She tried not to flinch away, even though he smelled less than freshly bathed.

'You've got it with you?'

She took the diary out of her bag and held it out. He snatched it from her, but then did not open it immediately. Almost as if he was afraid to. Then he gave a sob and said, 'Oh, Helen, I'm so sorry. I didn't mean it. I didn't mean to hurt you.'

Alarmed, Natalia tensed herself, measuring the distance to the front door. If only there were stairs nearby, not a lift to wait for or get trapped in. Then Peter pulled himself together. He wiped his nose with the back of his sleeve and, opening the clasp of the diary, began riffling through to the end. She saw his finger run down the page, then the next. There was a whole page to a day, a diary for writing in, not just noting appointments. Some pages were covered in writing, others only had a few lines. She looked away, not wanting to further invade Helen's privacy. She waited for him to get to that fateful Friday.

Peter gave a groan, and let the diary slip to the floor. This is why she'd waited; to witness his response. As he buried his head in his hands, all she could see were his shoulder's shaking with sobs.

She waited awkwardly for him to stop, but when that didn't happen, she began doing the talking. 'In order to get your address, Peter, I had to call your office. Can you guess who I spoke to there?'

His shoulders still shaking, Peter lifted his head. 'Yes ... Tanya.'

'Yes, Tanya Parsons. TP. I confronted her with the evidence of the diary, and she confessed that it was her who Helen had arranged to meet. That's why Helen threw the vase at you that morning. She suspected Tanya and you were having an affair, but she was waiting for confirmation. She didn't want to accuse you until she was sure. Tanya crumbled as soon as I confronted her. She confessed to telling your wife but, when she went missing, she kept quiet for fear of the repercussions.'

Peter's hand clamped onto her arm and she jumped violently. What was he going to do? His face was contorted with emotion. Was it conceivable his wife had come home and confronted him with his wrongdoing, they'd rowed, only this time there was more than broken glass to clear up? Somehow Natalia doubted this. There was so much pain in Peter, but still she needed to be guarded.

'I took the coward's way out. I see it all now,' he moaned. 'It's true. If only I hadn't done it! Why didn't Helen talk to me? I'd have explained that it meant nothing.' Peter let go of her arm, stood up and walked unsteadily to the sideboard. 'A shot of brandy, that's what I need. Want one?' He cracked open a fresh bottle, and it clinked against the rims of the cut-glass tumblers as he poured several inches of brandy into each without waiting for Natalia's reply. He put the glasses down in front of them and collapsed on the settee, taking a large gulp of the golden liquid, seemingly lost in his own thoughts. Then he began to speak, still in that slow, depressed way.

'It's funny. The thing you dread most happens. You'll do anything to stop it happening, and then, when it's out in the open, it's a strange kind of release.'

Natalia prayed he was talking about the affair coming to light and nothing more sinister. 'What was that thing, Peter?' she asked, trying not to sound fearful.

'The affair. The affair... If you can even call it that.

'It happened on one of those nights when Helen and I were falling apart, because Helen had just found out she wasn't pregnant again. I was working late, partly to earn extra money for the IVF, partly to get away from the strain at home. Tanya, she seemed so sympathetic. I didn't mean it to happen. It was uncomplicated, sex without babies or blame.

'It only happened a couple of times. I couldn't stand the guilt, and it felt wrong, anyway, being with her and not Helen. I thought it was the same for Tanya, a one-night stand or two.' He stopped and gulped some more brandy. Natalia drank some of hers and coughed as it caught her throat.

'Helen did not suspect?'

'No, I'm sure she didn't. She had no reason to. I tried to avoid being alone with Tanya after that.'

'It was not a one-night stand for Tanya, though.'

'No. She'd leave me messages, tried to keep a dialogue going. I thought if I kept away from her it would all fizzle out.'

'But Tanya wouldn't let go. She arranged to meet Helen, to tell her all about it.'

Peter looked at her, nursing the tumbler in his hands. 'How do you know all this?'

'I remembered meeting Tanya Parsons in your office. At the time I thought she was just concerned for you, nosy too perhaps. When I read that Helen was meeting her, I saw her behaviour from another angle, the way she tried to touch you. I worked out you'd had an affair. That is why Helen left.'

Instead of agreeing with her, Peter stared down at his brandy glass.

'Isn't it? Or is there something else?'

Peter bowed his head. Brandy spilled from the glass onto the rug. 'Could she have told her? Could Tanya have gone that far? Is that why? Because of the baby?'

'A baby?' This Natalia had not expected.

He jumped up and began to pace about, talking jerkily. 'A few weeks ago she told me. Tanya. That she was pregnant. She began to put pressure on me. Why did I stay with Helen? We couldn't have children. She, Tanya, could give me what I wanted. She used what I'd told her in confidence to try and manipulate me. I was such a fool. I'd assumed she was taking contraception.

'There was no one I could tell, no one I could share it with. Helen and I were closer than ever again, and I certainly couldn't tell her, not in her fragile state. It was a living nightmare. I told Tanya I would pay child maintenance, but nothing more was on offer. After all, it might not even be mine.

'I met with Tanya after work and begged her to keep quiet. I told her it was Helen I loved. She said that would change once we were together and that I only stayed with Helen because I felt sorry for her. I argued with her, said something I shouldn't about wanting a paternity test. That must have tipped her over the edge.'

'So Tanya arranged to meet Helen to tell her.'

'That must be it.' Peter fell silent, then continued. 'Since the Friday she disappeared I've been living on a knife edge. Did she

254

know? Was that why she'd left? I wondered why the row we'd had that morning was so intense. Oh, poor Helen.'

'You didn't ask Tanya outright whether she'd talked to Helen?'

'I guess it was always in the back of my mind, but when I did confront her with the possibility, she denied knowing anything about it, demanding to know what kind of woman I took her for. Hah!'

Natalia had no words of comfort for him. Two people who loved each other had been savaged and driven apart by circumstances beyond their control. Peter's response had been only too human. A brief dalliance. But the subsequent cost had been too high. Natalia could not imagine what pain Helen must have felt. She could not bear herself and her husband the child they longed for, but in a brief encounter – maybe embellished as more by Tanya – he'd impregnated someone else. How that must have turned the knife in the wound.

Peter straightened up. 'I'd better get this to the police. Tell them what I've told you.' He grimaced. 'It'll be music to DS Kane's ears. Husband cheats, wife leaves him. She was right all along.'

'Helen loved you once,' Natalia said tentatively. 'Once she's had a chance to absorb this blow, she might come back.'

'And Tanya might offer to let me and

Helen adopt her baby. Believe me I've had all these fantasies and more.'

Natalia heard the beep of a text message on her phone. She got it out, expecting it to be from Dermot. It was from Oman. She read it disbelievingly, out loud to Peter. 'HB traced to Watford, arrived 16.05 day of disappearance.'

'Watford?' he repeated. 'What was she doing all the way out there? Why would she travel to Watford?'

'Nothing to do with your IVF or doctors? Does she have friends out there?'

'No, not at all – oh, wait a minute. But no, I can't believe it.'

'What have you remembered?'

'My aunt and uncle live on the outskirts of Watford. They don't have children. We visit them very occasionally, to see they're all right.' He thought for a moment. 'But why would she go there? They're away, I'm sure of it. My sister told me – cruise of a lifetime, to Antarctica.'

They looked at one another.

'Do you have their keys?'

'No, but an old lady lives next door to them and has a set. We've met her. She'd remember Helen.'

Natalia could imagine the highly sensitive Helen, taking antidepressants, needing somewhere quiet to crawl away to, like a wounded animal, to give herself time to heal.

'There's no time to waste – I'm going. It might be a long shot, but I have to find Helen.'

26

The blue Audi's tyres squealed as Peter Bookman slammed on the brakes just in time as a container lorry thundered towards them, blocking their entrance onto the M1.

'Be careful, Peter,' Natalia shouted. 'It won't help Helen if you have an accident on the way to Watford.'

Peter didn't look at her. His knuckles, where he was gripping the steering wheel, were white.

'I know what I'm doing,' he said grimly, gunning the engine. The car leapt forward, careening across two lanes to the furious horns of other motorists, into the outside lane. He pressed his foot onto the accelerator and she watched the speedometer creep up to ninety miles per hour.

Why had she insisted on coming, she thought, as, white-faced, she clung to the edge of her seat.

Ignoring her protests that he'd had too much to drink, Peter had grabbed up his keys and wallet and started to bundle her out of the flat.

'You can't drive to Watford in your state. You must call DS Kane,' she told him, as they travelled down in the lift, but he was adamant.

'I have to see Helen, I have to get to her,' he kept repeating over and over again.

The lift clanged open into the concrete underground car park beneath the apartment block. Natalia hurried along behind Peter. She saw headlights flash on a dark-blue Audi as he pressed the key fob. He hurried towards the car and she hurried after him. When they reached it, he practically pushed her away.

'I'm coming with you,' Natalia heard herself announce.

'What for?' he snarled. 'I don't need you. *We* don't need you.'

'If Helen is in your uncle's house, it's because she needed time, to be alone. To be away from you. Seeing you could trigger who knows what crisis.' She flung the words at him, wanting in that moment only to get in the car and be there for Helen.

Peter flung his hands into the air. 'I don't have time to argue. Get in if you're coming.'

He didn't even wait for her to put her seat belt on before reversing the car out of its slot at speed, and roaring out of the car park.

From then on, Natalia had felt she was on a fairground ride that had gone out of control. The traffic was already building up towards rush hour, but Peter drove at break-neck speed wherever possible. St John's Wood, Swiss Cottage, cursing as he forced his way up the Finchley Road. He overtook a queue of cars by going into the oncoming lane and nearly causing an accident as he pushed his way back into the northbound flow of traffic. Natalia caught glimpses of rows of shops, then houses, then shops again. Pavements were filled with parents taking children home from school, with families carrying bags of shopping. She flinched every time she saw a child near the edge of a pavement. At any moment Peter might lose control and mount the kerb. At the speed he was driving, no one would escape injury.

'You may be an expert driver, but I'll be sick if we go around another bend like that,' she'd called out, exasperated, as he flung the car around a corner as a light turned from amber to red. 'You'll kill someone if you don't slow down.'

'I know what I'm doing,' Peter said.

'Have you thought what you're going to say to Helen when you get there?'

Now he did turn to look at her. His eyes had that intense look she'd seen before. 'Say to her? What do you mean?'

'Peter! The lorry!' Natalia closed her eyes as Peter swerved the car violently to avoid the supermarket delivery lorry bearing down on them. Thank goodness there was a metal fence along the side of the road, to protect pedestrians from the busy A41. When she opened her eyes he was staring fixedly ahead again, muttering to himself.

The sign for Golders Green had flashed by, then the towers of Brent Cross Shopping Centre. The North Circular Road bore away to their right, but Peter's speed was relentless, until the traffic began to crawl.

'Come on, come on!' he muttered, banging his palm against the steering wheel.

'Where are we now?' she asked.

'Staples Corner – I'm taking the M1. We could stay on the A road but this'll be faster at this time of day. If we can get onto it.'

And that was the moment when she was sure they must surely crash, as the Audi shot across those lanes onto the M1 and he settled into ninety miles an hour, pushing the car right up behind each car in front, and flashing his light bullyingly and shouting, 'Get over, get over!' till they moved into the middle lane and they could shoot forward again.

She was suddenly acutely aware that no one knew she was in the car with Peter Bookman, speeding who knew where. She only had his word for it that they were driving to Watford, that he would stop when he got there, and that he did have an uncle and aunt who lived there. She glanced at her watch. They'd been in the car for half an hour now.

'When do you think we'll get there?' she asked. 'My mobile's in my handbag. Why don't I phone your uncle's number and leave a message to warn Helen we're coming, if she doesn't answer—'

'How the hell can I remember what my uncle's bloody number is?' he shouted. 'There's no time to waste.'

'The address, give me the address.'

'It's twenty-five ... twenty-five, oh, I'll remember the way. Let me drive!'

'Then I will let DS Kane know that we are—'

'Helen won't want the police. No.'

'Why not, Peter?'

He suddenly stamped on the brakes. The tyres squealed mercilessly as they shuddered to a halt just in time as cars, vans and juggernauts all jammed on their brakes. Natalia swallowed bile rising in her throat. 'What's going on?'

'Junction interchange and speed cameras.'

She saw a sign for Scratchwood services coming up.

'Then let me call a doctor.'

'No,' he yelled. 'Helen will be all right. She'll see me, and we'll talk and—'

The car lurched forward, screaming ahead, Peter pumping the accelerator hard in low gear as he zigzagged between lanes, trying to gain an advantage till they were past the blockage. Natalia clung to the seat again, feet pressing into the well, hoping to find an imaginary brake pedal.

'Doctors, police, why not?' He was muttering to himself again in a low tone. 'Go on. Why not let the whole world know what an evil bastard I am.'

Natalia's unease turned to alarm. 'I'll just phone my husband,' she said, reaching for her mobile.

'No,' he said, pushing at her arm. 'Keep your eyes on the road.'

'Let me!' she said, in the firmest voice she could summon.

'Go on then,' he said. 'But he can't help us. This is between Helen and me.'

'I have to let him know I can't pick the children up from school,' she said, hoping the mention of children might bring a change in him. 'Nuala and Connor. Nuala is in the school Christmas play and–'

'Phone your husband.'

As Natalia searched in her bag, she began to hyperventilate.

Her mobile wasn't there.

Oh, you stupid girl, she cursed herself. *You must have left it in Peter Bookman's apartment.*

But a far more terrible thought crouched at the back of her mind. What if Peter had taken it?

She glanced at the male figure driving the

car. His forehead was shiny with sweat, and dark patches had stained his T-shirt. Supposing he had killed Helen? Supposing she had contacted him after meeting Tanya and, after travelling on the underground, they'd had such a terrible scene that he'd killed her and hidden the body? The posters, the pleading, it could all be an act, playing the grieving husband. Hadn't he just called himself an evil bastard?

She, Natalia, knew too much. Did he intend to do away with her, too, now, to keep her quiet? She looked out at lumbering traffic, picking up speed again. There were hedges, a field, houses in the distance. She was far away from all she knew, all she was familiar with. She must not betray her fear.

'Have you thought what you are going to say to Helen when you see her? You must be prepared that she might not want to see you or speak to you.'

'*If* I see her. How do we know she's there? Your colleague is sending us to Watford. Or so you say.'

Was he trying to undermine her, blaming her, to justify his actions? What would he do next?

'Omar is very careful – one of the top CCTV specialists in London. He wouldn't make a mistake...'

'Oh, and I do, you're saying. Yes, blame me. It's all my fault.' Suddenly his voice cracked. 'You can't blame me any more than I'm blaming myself.' Furiously he brushed his hand across his eyes, then grabbed hold of the steering wheel again. 'Six, junction six, that's the one we want. Garton side of Watford.'

Natalia stared ahead into the gathering gloom. She saw the sign for junction six. They were nearly there, despite Peter's best efforts to wreck the car.

But Natalia was worried about what they'd find.

27

Now they'd left the madness of the motorway and major roads, Peter drove more slowly through residential streets. He drew up outside a white-painted, mock-Tudor semi-detached house, dating from the 1930s, with garden at the front and rear. It was getting dark, and the curtains were drawn. Was Peter going to try and force her into this house, she wondered? Natalia looked around for any sign of another person – there were a few lighted windows, but no people in sight.

'Get out,' he said. 'We're here.'

Legs wobbling slightly, she climbed out, shut the car door, and began to follow him up the path. Then she thought she could see a glimmer of light through the stained-glass panel in the front door and a movement caught Natalia's eye.

'Helen!' she cried out involuntarily, her fear disappearing in a flash.

The curtain in the front window had been lifted a few inches. A woman's face appeared there, looking ghostly. Then the curtain was dropped.

'It's Helen, she's all right. Thank God.' Peter ran towards the front door and pressed the doorbell, keeping his forefinger on so it rang continuously.

'Helen, it's me, Peter. Are you all right?'

She did not come to the front door. There was no sign of movement inside. He took his finger off the bell and bent to the letterbox. 'Helen, I just want you to speak to me for a moment, tell me how you are, if you need anything. You don't have to let me in if you don't want to. Talk to me through the letterbox, that will do.' He rattled the letterbox, and pushed at the door a couple of times.

No one stirred inside the house.

'Let me call the police,' Natalia suggested, as Peter knocked at the door, calling out, 'Come on, Helen darling, please talk to me for a few moments, then I'll leave you in peace.'

'Go away!' came a high-pitched scream

from within. 'I don't want to see you.'

'You don't have to see me. Just talk to me.'

'You're not coming in!'

'I don't want to come in. I just want to talk.' But he confounded his words by banging and pushing at the front door.

'Stop ... stop!' came the voice from within.

This was what Natalia had feared. She longed to have Dermot with her. Anyone, in fact. She laid a restraining hand on Peter's arm. 'You'll frighten Helen,' she said.

'But I want to talk. Explain.' He slapped at the wood in frustration.

'Helen may not want to hear what you have to say.'

As if to support her words they heard. 'I can't bear it! I can't bear it!' There was another thin scream from inside, as if Helen's voice was hoarse, followed by the sound of something falling over then feet running up stairs.

Peter turned to her. 'We have to get in!'

Before Natalia could say anything, he ran round to the back of the house, and she followed him. He was trying the back door, but it was locked. Then they both saw the kitchen window was ajar. In a matter of moments, he'd wrenched it open and was climbing inside, knocking crockery to the floor as he did so. He then unlocked the back door so that she could enter.

Peter switched on the kitchen light and

they looked around. The sink was cluttered with dirty dishes and the pedal bin was overflowing with the discarded wrappers and cartons of frozen food. 'This isn't Helen,' he groaned. 'This is because of me, all because of me.'

A door slammed above them. Peter ran out of the kitchen and began leaping up the stairs, stumbling in his haste and grabbing hold of the banisters. Natalia followed, glancing into the living room as she did so. In the light from the streetlamp outside she could make out blankets and a pillow on the sofa. On the floor beside it were cups and glasses. It looked as if Helen had been sleeping in there. There was a phone there, too. Natalia picked it up, and dialled Dermot's telephone number. It went straight to voice mail. She tried to compose her voice as she told him where she was. The thought of frightening her husband made her feel sick. She kept the message succinct.

After she'd put the phone down, she heard a heated exchange from upstairs, and made her way to the first floor. On the landing she could see that two doors were wide open, leading to bedrooms. The third was closed, and Peter was pounding on it. 'Helen, stop this, let me in.' He looked over his shoulder. 'She's locked herself in the bathroom.'

'Go away. I hate you, I hate you,' Helen's voice was choked with emotion. They could hear the sound of cabinets being opened and things falling on the floor. 'I may as well kill myself. There's no point in going on any more.' She finished on a wailing note.

Natalia knew that she must do something. On her own in the house, Helen had managed to live in suspension, in limbo, keeping all her troubles at arm's length. Peter's arrival had punctured her safe cocoon, allowing painful emotions to flood back in and she was finding them intolerable.

'Go and see if you can find a ladder to reach the bathroom,' she said. 'And check around the house for Helen's tablets. You know what they look like. Or anything else she may have taken in there with her. And call an ambulance, too.' She kept her voice firm and low.

He looked at her with a terrified expression, but didn't move.

'An ambulance?'

'Go!' she ordered.

Peter broke out of his spell and dashed downstairs.

Calling again on her past training Natalia knocked gently on the bathroom door. 'Hello, Helen, my name's Natalia, Natalia O'Shea. Your husband's gone downstairs now. There's only me outside.'

A muffled sob came from inside. 'I don't care who you are. You could be another of his ... his women.'

'I work for the Lost Property Office, in Baker Street. Your scarf and shoes and bag were handed in to us. Do you remember leaving them on the Circle Line train?' She spoke as soothingly as she could.

'Oh yes, the Circle Line.' Helen spoke almost dreamily. 'I remember that. I had to get away, leave my old things behind. Then people would think I was dead, and forget about me. I may as well be dead.' She started weeping again, great wrenching sobs and there was a rattling noise. Natalia tried to identify it. Could she be shaking a pill bottle? Who knew what medication Peter's aunt and uncle might have in their bathroom cabinet, which might react badly with Helen's anti-depressants. Downstairs, she could hear Peter talking to the Emergency Operator. She must keep Helen talking.

'I'm here to listen, if you would like to talk to me about it. That day, and what happened.'

'What good's talking? It's all over. All done. No reason to anything any more.' Then she shouted the last two words. 'No reason!'

Natalia heard her turning a tap on. Was she running water so that she could take some pills?

'I'd like to hear about it, Helen. Why is everything over?'

'My marriage, my trust – my life.'

Natalia laid her hand flat on the door, reaching out. 'Trust is hard to rebuild, but it can be done. People have done it. There is always hope,' she said cautiously.

There was the sound of something smashing, then a thud. 'Hope? There is no hope. None at all. I don't care about hope. I don't care about trust. I don't care about anything any more.' Her words were agonised. 'My life is finished.'

'You feel your life is finished,' Natalia affirmed. 'Why is it finished?'

'All these questions. Because ... because it has no purpose any more.' Helen fell silent then, as Natalia was about to speak, added in a low voice, 'I can't have children. I'm useless, barren, I shouldn't live. Go away and let me die. And that woman. That *she* should have his child. That *she* should be able to walk off into the sunset with him. It's all so wrong. So wrong. What did I do to deserve this?'

'The loss feels unbearable. I know,' Natalia sighed and sank down onto the floor, leaning her back against the door. 'It happened to me, too.'

There was a silence, a sniff. 'You can't have children, either?'

'I ... lost my child. My only son.' Natalia felt her grief anew, as raw as the first day.

'I'm sorry.' There were sounds from inside, as if Helen was lowering herself to the floor. Had she taken some medication? Worse, had she cut herself? Where was the ambulance? Perhaps she should let Peter break down the door now. Before she was afraid it would make Helen overreact. Now, it might be needed to save her life. 'To have a baby and lose it. That's terrible. Was he ill?'

'My husband was from Turkey. His family wanted us to go and live there, but I ... I was not ready to leave. We fought. He stole my son.' It sounded so stark, said like that. It could not convey the pain and heartache on all sides.

'How long ago?' Helen's voice was quieter now.

'Six years.'

'I don't know ... which is worse. To lose your child ... or never to be able to have one.' Helen panted between her words.

Natalia closed her eyes. 'At first I thought I couldn't bear it. I tried every way to find him. But you know, after a while you find a strength from somewhere. A strength you never knew you had.'

'Never knew you had,' Helen repeated softly.

Natalia remembered then what it was that had drawn her into the search for Helen. The sadness in her eyes on that poster Peter had created. It was a reflection of her own sadness.

'There are good days and there are bad days. But you find you can go on. It's amazing what the human spirit can endure.'

'Ah, but ... you must be very strong... I'm weak ... only child. Spoiled. Protected. I don't know how ... to carry on.'

Peter appeared on the stairs behind her, and the wildness in his eyes was gone. Natalia held her finger to her lips, and thankfully he was silent.

'We each find our own way. Helen, can you hear me Helen?'

'I can hear you,' Helen whispered. 'I feel so lonely. I'm so alone. It's all black and ... there's only me. I can't bear it.'

'We're all alone in some ways,' Natalia said. 'But we're all loved.'

'No one loves me. Why should they? I'm useless.'

Natalia remembered how Helen's mother had phoned Peter and the police several times a day, asking about her daughter. She thought she could hear sounds from below, and redoubled her efforts to keep Helen with her.

'Your mum,' she said. 'She's been beside herself with worry about you.' She pressed her ear to the door and thought she heard Helen draw in a breath. 'She's been phoning every day. Desperate for news of you. You were her little girl. The girl she hugged and kissed and brought up.'

Natalia heard Helen's rasping breathing – and then, the distant, but welcome wail of an ambulance siren.

'I'm sorry. I phoned but couldn't ... couldn't tell her. I was ashamed. Didn't want to worry her. Didn't want her to know that she couldn't ... that we can't have the grandchildren she always wanted.'

Peter began to cry quietly, too, and Natalia watched him slide down the wall, his fist at his mouth.

'Helen, listen to me. Your mum loves you. If she were to lose you, her pain would be unbearable, just like you're feeling now. Stay with me, Helen. Keep fighting.'

The doorbell rang. Peter jumped to his feet and headed down the stairs. Helen started wailing in huge, ragged moans that became wrenching sobs. The sort of sobs that Natalia recognised came from deep within. But they were also the first step towards healing. Helen had sunk to the bottom, tried to avoid the worst moment of grief, but without going through it you couldn't come through to the other side. The crisis point.

'Helen – can you come to the door? Can you open the door? Then we can ring your mum and you can speak to her.'

She heard fumbling sounds, then the key being turned in the lock.

'I can't, I can't open it,' Helen whispered.

At the same time there were sounds from the stairs behind her and a balding, burly man in a fluorescent jacket appeared at her side. He was carrying a holdall, which he placed on the carpet as he knelt beside Natalia.

'It's OK. I'll take over. I'm a paramedic. I'm Mike. Mike the bike they call me. Let's see, Helen, isn't it?'

'Yes,' came the reply.

'Helen, I need you to stand well back from the door. Can you do that for me, love?'

Natalia heard her shifting behind the door, and Mike took the handle in one hand.

'Are you well away from the door, Helen?'

'Yes,' she said.

Mike took a step back, then slammed his considerable bulk against the bathroom door. The lock splintered, but the door didn't fly open. He pushed it open gently.

Natalia looked in. Helen was half supine on the bathroom floor under the sink. Packets and bottles of medication were scattered around her. There was no blood. Her eyelids fluttered as her eyes rolled up.

'OK, what have you been taking here. Uh uh, what a cocktail. Helen, stay with me, can you hear me?' As Helen mumbled, he asked Natalia, 'Fetch my bag will you? I've got something in there that'll make her throw up these things. How long has it been?'

Natalia had lost any sense of time. 'A few

minutes? Five?' She turned to get his bag and found Peter standing there holding it out to her. He was gazing humbly at Helen. 'May I go to her?'

Helen's hair was matted, she wore no make-up and her clothes were all mismatched but he looked at her as if she were the most beautiful person on the earth.

'That's up to Mike,' she said, as the paramedic got to work.

At that moment, Helen opened her eyes. 'Tell Mum, I love her.' And then was violently sick.

Natalia padded slowly downstairs, feeling utterly exhausted. She went into the kitchen and picked up the kettle. Her hands trembled so much she could hardly hold it. The kettle bumped against the tap and cold water shot over her top. She put it on its mat and pressed the lever on. Then she leaned on the work surface. A cup of tea to calm the nerves. What a time, she thought, attempting a weak smile, to show how British she had become.

Epilogue

'Gangway, gangway.' Avon was jabbing at Natalia's back with a tray. She stepped aside to let her deposit her plates of sausage rolls, mince pies and cheesy biscuits. Two desks had been put together to make a long-enough space to put out the food and drink for the LPO Christmas party. Natalia had brought the Polish biscuits she'd made herself, though she knew they wouldn't be as good as her grandmother's. Cliff had brought a quiche, Mark lemonade and beer, and the others sandwiches and crisps. There was a Christmas cake decorated with icing and topped with tiny snowmen. Would they ever be able to eat all this stuff?

'Come on, Natalia, don't just stand there, get those plastic cups out for the drinks.'

'Yes, Avon.' Natalia raised her eyes heavenward. Just when she thought she and Avon were on an even footing, Avon contrived a way to boss her about again.

'Yes, come along, Natalia, stop pretending it's a festive holiday and get to work,' Mark scolded, in a weak impersonation of Avon's shrill contralto. Natalia laughed and went to fetch the plastic cups from Avon's desk, then stood them in a row in front of the food. Just as she'd finished, she felt a presence behind her.

'Stefan, what's that!' she protested.

'Mistletoe. It means I can kiss any girl I want. I just hold it over her head. Great idea!' He kissed her gently on the cheek. 'Now who else can I grab?'

'How about me?' said Avon, appearing at Stefan's side. Natalia never knew she could move so fast and slid away, trying to keep a straight face. Stefan had met his match there!

They had decorated the office with paper chains and a small plastic Christmas tree stood on an empty desk. Cards from other departments and grateful members of the public were pinned up on the noticeboard, a colourful display of holly and robins and jolly snow scenes.

'It's four o'clock,' Avon called out. 'Poppy, you go and look after reception, the rest of you, it's party time.'

Poppy, the most junior member of staff, headed for reception.

'I'll bring you a plate of food,' Mark said to her as she passed and she flashed him a pretty smile.

Natalia saw him turn pink for the first time ever.

Cliff emerged from the vault and stood uncertainly looking on. His small eyes had not brightened at the prospect of all the food, unlike the young men, who were already piling their plates high.

'Here's the wine. Pour it out, Natalia.'

She filled the plastic cups with not-very-cold white wine and handed them round. Then they all stood in a circle. Natalia found herself longing for Rasheda, who would surely banish the uncomfortable smiles and shuffling of feet and get the party going.

Donna at last left her office and strode over. 'I'd like to say a few words,' she said. 'First of all, it looks like we've seen the last of the Hoaxer, thanks to everyone's vigilance. Of course, that's not to say the culprit won't reoffend in future, but it seems he, or she, has been scared off for now.' She did not look in Natalia's direction. 'Secondly, I've just heard from the office inspectors. Manchester is no longer the best lost property office in the country. We are! Congratulations, everybody and help yourselves to some sparkling wine.'

Her secretary, Rose, appeared carrying a tray of champagne flutes while Donna produced two bottles of chilled Cava. Stefan stepped forward. 'I'm very good at this,' he said, and began easing the corks out. Everyone cowered down, expecting the corks to go off with a bang, but he managed it like a professional waiter, with a light pop, and no spillage.

'Here's to us,' Donna said, holding up her

glass. They all cheered and the ice was broken. Natalia had been feeling Cliff's speculative gaze on her, especially when Donna had mentioned the demise of the Hoaxer, but he did not come over.

'When is your flight home?' she asked Stefan.

His face lit up. 'Ten o'clock tonight. Stansted,' he made a face. 'But very cheap. After today, prices go sky high until after New Year.'

'Have a wonderful time with your family.'

'Thank you.' They were both quiet for a moment, and Natalia assumed that Stefan, like she, was visualising the very different festive celebrations that would take place in their native countries.

'That Mr Bookman was giving you hard time. I hope he is very grateful now. You found his wife.'

'What are these?' Avon thrust a plate between Stefan and Natalia.

'Pierniki. Polish spice biscuits. We have them at Christmas. I made them myself.'

'They're very good.' To prove his point, Stefan took two and popped them both in his mouth.

'Hmm,' Avon said and tentatively bit into one. 'Not bad.'

'Thank you for your hairdresser recommendation,' Natalia said. Avon had given her the name of a stylist, who had put lowlights into her sleek new style. 'Even Nuala says my hair is OK.'

Avon waved a hand, then embarked on a long story to Stefan. Natalia moved away. She and Avon might never be friends, but at least they had a truce of sorts.

'Why do we have to have our party so early?' Mark complained, wandering by.

Avon turned on him. 'Because Stefan has a plane to catch and he didn't want to miss the party.'

'You mean *you* didn't want to miss catching *him* under the mistletoe,' Mark winked to Natalia.

'Looking forward to Christmas?' asked Donna, joining her.

'We're going to a Christmas carol concert tonight at a local church, and many other good things. My first Christmas in London – it'll be great. We already saw the school show – Nuala was great in that. And you?'

'I'm staying with friends in the country. They've got a big estate in Dorset. No children. It'll be a very grown-up Christmas. A big house party.'

'Any policemen going?' Natalia asked, smiling.

'There just might be one special one. Fingers crossed.' Donna winked.

Emboldened by her second glass of Cava, Natalia asked, 'Tell me, Donna, what's so special about the Special Items room? Cliff won't tell me!'

Donna's eyes sparkled. 'I bet he hasn't. He's so old-fashioned! It's where we put the, ahem, "marital aids".'

Natalia wasn't familiar with the term and frowned.

'Sex toys!' said Donna. 'And other things – naughty magazines and stuff like that. You'd be amazed at what people leave lying about. It's some old tradition from the 1950s to keep them locked away. I'm glad you mentioned it. I think we'll do away with that locked door. Especially as I know that Cliff uses it for a crafty smoke when it's raining outside.'

As they laughed together, Natalia again felt Cliff watching her. She wondered if he enjoyed the reading matter in there while having his cigarette.

'And what happens when these things reach their three-month, end-of-storage date? I suppose people are too shy to come and claim them.'

'You'd be surprised how bold some people are. But I tell you now, I'm not starting a charity with them, that's for sure!'

Natalia looked round at her new-found friends. Yes, for that's what they were, despite their peculiarities and their ups and downs. Shaking her head, she swallowed her wine and pulled on her coat.

'Happy Christmas everyone,' she called

out. 'I have to leave now. Bye!'

A chorus of voices tried to persuade her to stay, then wished her well when she protested that she couldn't.

As she left the building, going out into a frosty Baker Street, breath misting in front of her, she heard Cliff hurrying to catch her up.

'You and Donna seem very pally these days,' he said without preamble, reverting to his normal crusty demeanour. 'Is that something to do with the end of the Hoaxer?'

'And hello to you, too, Cliff,' she said. 'I saw you keeping an eye on us. Donna is pleased I helped find Helen Bookman. It's kudos for the Lost Property Office. You know how ambitious she is. You helped find Helen, too.'

'Aye, well,' he gave a grudging smile. 'I just think it's very odd. No more hoaxes, Donna preening herself – I'm sure you know more than you're saying, but you're a discreet lassie. Good at keeping secrets.'

'You are getting to know me well, Cliff,' she said, smiling. 'I hope you have a good Christmas. I have a few days off now, so I'll see you in the New Year.'

Natalia thought she saw the inkling of a smile beneath Cliff's bushy beard, and felt a sudden concern for him. What did the festive season hold for him, she wondered. A microwaved Christmas lunch on his knee, alone, watching the Queen's speech? She felt the sudden need to invite him to their home, but imagining the look on Dermot's face stopped herself saying anything of the sort.

'Where will you be spending Christmas, Cliff?'

He hesitated, and shuffled his feet nervously.

'I do a bit of voluntary work, young deprived kids, boys and girls. Sports training, basketball, boxing mainly. I was a sports instructor once over and I've kept my hand in. Some of the parents are putting on a party and I'm invited.'

'Good for you, Cliff. Take care now.'

As she turned into the station entrance she nearly tripped over Homeless Joe, who gave her a smile and a nod. He waggled his feet, drawing attention to the very fine pair of Timberland walking boots he now wore. The first distribution of shoes had gone out this week, in time for Christmas – another PR coup for Donna Harris of the Lost Property Office.

She hurried down to the platform, and squeezed into an almost-full carriage.

A few hours later she was sitting next to Dermot in St Michael's near to their house. The church had close links with Nuala's school, so the audience was filled with parents, assorted relatives and friends. The congregation settled into an expectant hush as the choir filed in to take their places in the stalls.

As the first notes rang out, Natalia thought of Helen. She'd visited her just once, in hospital, the day after that terrifying drive to Watford. Face pale and drawn, that rich hair fanned out on the pillow, she'd barely been able to speak, she was so heavily tranquillised. But she'd smiled and held Natalia's hand. Peter sat at her other side, clutching her other hand.

'She's doing very well,' Natalia had told Dermot afterwards. 'She's even able to face Peter again, and he's visiting her every day. And her mum goes in all the time, too.'

'Truly a case of lost and found there, Natalia,' Dermot had said. 'The poor woman was driven nearly demented that she couldn't have a baby.'

As he spoke, Natalia saw the uncertainty in his face and knew what would come next.

'We're so lucky, you and I. We know we can have children. Wouldn't it be grand to have one of our very own.'

His eyes were so full of kindness, but her heart had felt torn in pieces. She was drawn in one direction by Dermot's yearning – and yes, her own, too, it was dawning on her. And yet she was held back, dragged in another direction by the memory of Paul. Her son whom she'd failed to keep. Who was still lost to her. Why the sense of betrayal?

She'd looked at Dermot, and could do nothing to stop the tears in her eyes.

'I wish but ... not yet, I don't think I can, not yet.'

As always Dermot's hug was warm and understanding. She did not allow herself a further fear, how far could she test his love?

Thankfully, he changed the subject. 'Have you thought about Omar's offer – a change of career?'

Natalia sniffed a little. 'It was lovely to be asked, and the work would be interesting, I'm sure. But my place is in Lost Property.'

The first carol was over, and Miss Ogwala, one of the teachers at Nuala's school, stood at the lectern to read a poem. Natalia fingered the letter in her handbag she'd received from her Fatima. She'd written back. A request for some kind of contact, a webcam link, a phone call now and then – with a promise, even though it broke her heart to do so – that she wouldn't steal him away.

But just to see her Paul again, know him, see him grow. Then, she hoped, she too could feel she'd found herself again, and could start to look forward once more.

The publishers hope that this book has given you enjoyable reading. Large Print Books arc especially designed to be as easy to see and hold as possible. If you wish a complete list of our books please ask at your local library or write directly to:

Dales Large Print Books
Magna House, Long Preston,
Skipton, North Yorkshire.
BD23 4ND

This Large Print Book, for people
who cannot read normal print,
is published under the auspices of

THE ULVERSCROFT FOUNDATION

... we hope you have enjoyed this book.
Please think for a moment about those
who have worse eyesight than you ...
and are unable to even read or enjoy
Large Print without great difficulty.

You can help them by sending a
donation, large or small, to:

**The Ulverscroft Foundation,
1, The Green, Bradgate Road,
Anstey, Leicestershire, LE7 7FU,
England.**
or request a copy of our brochure for
more details.

The Foundation will use all donations
to assist those people who are visually
impaired and need special attention
with medical research, diagnosis
and treatment.

Thank you very much for your help.